The car stopped.

Ryan opened her eyes and took in the red door of her condo, softly lit by the porch light she'd turned on when they'd left.

She looked into his eyes, wondering if she should voice her desire. With this next question there'd be no turning back.

"Would you like to come inside?"

Adam's smile was slight as he shook his head. "No. I want to go home."

Her heart fell. A man like Adam? She should have known. She gathered her purse and made a move for the door.

Strong fingers clamped around her arm, holding her fast. "Wait! I want you to come with me so that we can...finish what we've started. Would you like that?"

Ryan laid her head on his shoulder. "I'd love that."

Ryan closed her eyes as she felt Adam's lips against her temple, his hand stroking her hair. Those blasted whispers tried to push through the haze of happiness and warn her that she was just being used and would then be tossed away. She shut her mind and refused to listen. She was a twenty-first-century woman who knew what she wanted. If in fact Adam was using her, so be it. Because tonight she planned to put his hard, strong body to good use, too.

* * *

Ready for the Rancher is part of the Sin City Secrets series.

Dear Reader,

Seriously...is there anything sexier than a cowboy? Hat tipped low. Jeans riding lower. Boots well-worn or shiny and new. Rugged demeanor. Swagger for days.

You all have my dad, grandfather and brother to thank for Adam's story. Like many of you, many of my teen days were spent between the pages of a romance I'd "borrowed" from my sister's collection. But, my first Western was by Louis L'Amour, an author my brother loved. To this day, my dad watches reruns of *Bonanza* and *The Big Valley*.

The place to fantasize about my own stallion was down in Arkansas on my grandparents' farm. There were no thoroughbred horses. No peacocks, manicured lawns and gargantuan estates like you'll find in the Breedlove's world, but there was hard work and deep love. There were shotguns and a grandma who knew how to use them. And, there were acres and acres of land, the perfect backdrop for dreaming. Here's to you becoming a DayDreamer, too!

Enjoy, and have a zuriday.com!

Zuri

ZURI DAY

—

READY FOR THE RANCHER

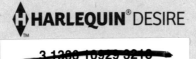

HARLEQUIN®DESIRE

Recycling programs
for this product may
not exist in your area.

ISBN-13: 978-1-335-60394-4

Ready for the Rancher

Copyright © 2019 by Zuri Day

This edition published by arrangement with Harlequin Books S.A.

For questions and comments about the quality of this book,
please contact us at CustomerService@Harlequin.com.

® and TM are trademarks of Harlequin Enterprises Limited or its
corporate affiliates. Trademarks indicated with ® are registered in the
United States Patent and Trademark Office, the Canadian Intellectual
Property Office and in other countries.

Printed in U.S.A.

Zuri Day is the national bestselling author of two dozen novels, including the popular Drakes of California series. She is a winner of the RSJ Emma Award, the AALAS (African American Literary Awards Show) Best Romance Award and others, and a finalist for multiple *RT Book Reviews* Best Book Awards in Multicultural Fiction. She wants you to have a zuriday.com!

Books by Zuri Day

Harlequin Desire

Sin City Secrets

Sin City Vows
Ready for the Rancher

Harlequin Kimani Romance

Champagne Kisses
Platinum Promises
Solid Gold Seduction
Secret Silver Nights
Crystal Caress

Visit her Author Profile page at Harlequin.com, or zuriday.com, for more titles.

You can find Zuri Day on Facebook, along with other Harlequin Desire authors, at Facebook.com/harlequindesireauthors!

At home on the range or a night on the town
Whether funky line dancing or lazing around.
This book is for the reader who likes to enjoy
A ride around Sin City and a sexy cowboy!

One

The same sounds that helped build the Breedlove empire worked Adam Breedlove's nerves, especially after putting in a twelve-hour day. Spinning wheels. Jangly music. Bells. Beeps. Chimes. Sounds that could be heard in any casino everywhere, even the virtual ones now online and accessible by almost anybody with a computer and an internet connection. Yet he took his time as he strolled through the loud, spacious area, two floors down and away from the CANN Casino Hotel and Spa's opulent, upscale and quiet main lobby. He was "keeping his feet in the grass," as his father would tell him. Staying close to the source of their great wealth was to always be reminded of who was really important—the CANN customer.

Before leaving the executive offices where Adam served as vice president of research and development for CANN International, he'd removed his suit jacket and tie and had rolled up the sleeves of his stark white shirt. It was a move to leave the position behind and appear casual, blending in with the patrons. He took in the vast Friday-night crowd, noted with satisfaction that a majority of the machines were occupied. He smiled and offered discreet waves to employees who recognized him. Eyes all across the room charted his progress. Some women offered flirty smiles. Others just stared. Men, too. Adam took it all in stride.

"Yo, Adam!"

Adam stopped and turned in the direction of the yell. A stocky man of average height waved as he walked toward him. The face looked familiar but...

"It's Dennis, man. Dennis Washington."

"Washboard?" Adam laughed and shook the hand Dennis extended.

Dennis patted his beer gut. "Not anymore."

"That's why I didn't recognize you! What's going on, man? I haven't seen you in forever."

"Since high school, no doubt."

"Where have you been? Still living here, in Las Vegas?" Adam began walking toward an exit leading from the casino into a quieter hallway, a small seating area and a bank of elevators. Dennis fell into step beside him.

He shook his head. "Bakersfield. The family moved there shortly after I graduated, and just before I left for the military. When I came back, I settled there. Felt it was as good a place as any."

"You were in the service?" Adam asked, his look one of teasing surprise. "I can't imagine anyone telling you what to do."

Dennis smiled. "It was an adjustment."

"How long were you in?"

"Four years." A pained expression flickered across his face. "That was enough."

"That's awesome, Dennis. Thank you for your service."

Dennis's response fit somewhere between a grunt and a snort. Adam didn't know what the sound meant, but he knew to leave it alone.

"Are you staying here, at the hotel?"

"No, this place is too rich for my blood." He took a long admiring glance around. "It's something else, though. You Breedloves always were a cut above the competition. But this place is cuts, plural."

Adam couldn't disagree. His family had made history when their company, CANN International, had built the first seven-star hotel in North America. It had become the hotel of choice for anyone who had money or clout. But he'd been at the hotel since early that morning. Right now he couldn't wait to get away from the place.

"An army buddy of mine has a place in Henderson. I'm crashing there," Dennis said.

They reached the elevators. Adam went to the one on the end, slid open a panel discreetly tucked next to the doors and placed his thumb on the scanner. "How long are you going to be here? It would be cool to catch up."

"I'd love that, bro, and would especially like to talk about your other business, Breedlove Ranch. I read that you breed cattle and are building your own processing plant."

Adam nodded. "You read correctly. It's almost completed."

"That's the industry I'm in."

"Oh, yeah?"

"Yep. I manage a slaughterhouse in Bakersfield, one of the largest in the state."

The elevator arrived. Its doors opened without a sound. Adam waved a hand over the door panel. The elevator doors remained open.

"No kidding. How long have you been doing that?" Adam asked.

"Been working at the plant since returning from the military eight years ago, managing it for the last four years."

"We should definitely talk. How long will you be here?"

"I'm flying back tomorrow night."

Adam pulled out his phone. "Give me your number." Dennis complied. "I'll give you a call. Maybe we can do lunch."

"Sounds like a plan."

After a hand grip and shoulder bump, the men parted ways.

The next morning, after confirming a meeting with Dennis via text, downing a quick breakfast and enjoying a ride on his prize stallion, Thunder, Adam jumped into his brand-spanking-new limited-edition pickup and headed into the downtown of Breedlove, Nevada. The unincorporated town of just over two thousand residents was founded more than twenty years ago by Adam's father, Nicholas, and a group of like-minded businessmen. It was about twenty-five miles northeast of the Las Vegas Strip, surrounded by mountains, with planned communities and a number of businesses in and around the quaint downtown square. Anchoring one corner of that square was a restaurant Adam owned called BBs, which stood for Breedlove Burgers, purchased specifically to showcase the beef raised at his ranch.

He reached the place and pulled into a crowded parking lot. An affordable menu, comfortable decor and stiff drinks had made the spot a favorite among the residents, especially the younger crowd. Adam drove around to the reserved parking at the back of the building and entered through the employee entrance.

"Hey, Adam!"

"*Hola*, Miguel." Adam gave a shoulder bump to the restaurant's head chef. *"Qué pasa, hombre?"*

"Nada, man." Miguel shook his head at what he jokingly called Adam's "gringo Spanish."

"You come here to work or what?"

"I came here to eat a good burger. Think I can get a table?"

"I don't know, boss. You might have to wait in line."

Adam spoke to and joked with other employees as he continued past the building's offices, through the kitchen and into the main dining room, where he spotted Dennis sitting at one of the tables by the window. What made Adam almost stop midstride and have to catch his breath was that his former high school friend wasn't alone. If heaven was missing an angel, Adam knew where God could find her. Sitting at his burger joint—BBs.

Ryan Washington felt nauseous, and not just her stomach was upset. When inviting her to lunch, Dennis knew the last place his vegetarian sister would want to eat was a burger joint. He wasn't the only one at fault. She should have known that Dennis's inviting her anywhere held an ulterior motive, came with strings attached. She'd grown up adoring her older sibling and while she'd wished otherwise, they'd never been super close. Heck, before his call that morning she hadn't even known he was in Las Vegas. At first she'd flat-out refused. For many reasons. She'd had a full day planned, a practice about to open. Then there was the very personal matter that she hadn't shared with her family. But as was often the case, Dennis had persuasively changed her mind. After admitting there was a little more to his request than just having lunch, he'd told her about meeting an old friend who was now very successful. That he hoped to do business with him and that her presence might help. When she asked why, he'd very politically incorrectly said, "Because my friend likes pretty girls."

That should have been enough to reinstate her refusal. Dennis wasn't generous with compliments. For her brother to call her pretty meant he really felt he needed her help. And hinting to set her up with one of his friends? Not in a million years. What kind of business was this? And what if said business meant he'd spend more time in Las Vegas?

So there she sat, handling what work she could by way of her cell phone, mentally blocking out odors and wanting the meeting to be over.

"There he is!"

Ryan looked up when her brother spoke, and momentarily froze. The man—or was it the brother of Adonis?—who returned Dennis's greeting was gorgeous, as though he'd stepped right out of a Wild West billboard ad and walked in for a meal. Everything about him screamed cowboy—Stetson hat, plaid shirt, snug-fitting denims and Western boots—all on a body for which it looked as though the clothes had been designed. *But a cowboy with clean, manicured nails?* That observation didn't fit with her assumption at all. That could never happen. Tall, dark and handsome was way too common a statement to use for the hunk in front of her. But it fit. He was toned and fine with close-cropped curls, dark, intense eyes and lips made for kissing. He smiled and revealed the knockout punch, a dimple. Ryan had always been a sucker for those.

For once, a temporarily speechless Ryan was grateful for her older brother's big mouth. She dropped her eyes down to her cell phone to call up composure and pull reasonable bits of calm and collected back from whatever part of her mind they'd fled.

"Good to see you," Dennis continued, as Hunkalicious sat down in one of two remaining wooden seats around the square table. "Couldn't believe when the waiter told us this was your place. Guess I shouldn't have been surprised, you running a cattle ranch and all. The server who seated us swore the burgers here were the best in the West. Didn't she, Ryan?"

Ryan meant to look at her brother, but of their own accord her eyes were drawn to the ones now boring into her with a casual intensity, deep chocolate orbs that fairly twinkled, framed by slightly arched eyebrows and long curly lashes.

She refocused on Dennis. "Yes, she did."

Actually Ryan hadn't been paying attention while Dennis flirted with the server. But since this guy her brother was trying to impress owned the establishment, she felt a little creative conversation was justified.

"You remember me talking about the Breedloves, right? The family who owns the CANN hotel on the Strip? This is one of the brothers, Adam. He and I went to high school together."

"Hello." Adam's smile was warm and genuine.

"Hi." Ryan suddenly felt shy, a rare occurrence. But she maintained eye contact.

"I don't think you ever met Ryan," Dennis continued.

"She's my kid sister. Growing up she was a nuisance. I rarely allowed her around."

Ryan's brow raised at her brother's comment. Not that it wasn't true. As a precocious eight-year-old with a newfound love for board games and sports, she'd followed her fearless, then-fourteen-year-old athletic big brother around like a puppy, wanted to be where he was and to do what he did. For him, it was so not cool.

"I can't imagine you being a nuisance." Adam held out his hand. "It's a pleasure to meet you."

His voice reminded her of how a good brandy tasted—earthy, spicy, with a warmth that burned gently on its way down. She took his hand and noted its softness. He may own a ranch, but this definitely wasn't a man who spent his days herding cattle or baling hay.

"Likewise," she replied.

It was the merest caress, just a light squeeze of the hand she placed in his. But for Ryan it transmitted all sorts of messages. That he was thoughtful and gentle, yet strong and secure. He was probably a fabulous lover. Ryan had no idea why the thought crossed her mind. She couldn't have cared less, but there was something about him…

Ryan wasn't the only one smitten. *Am I smitten? Surely not!* At least half a dozen other females within her line of vision were, and definitely their cute server with perfectly coiffed twists, who bounced up to their table wearing a smile as bright as her starched white shirt.

"Hey, Adam!"

"Hello, Zoe, a ray of sunshine, as always. Zoe is our top server," Adam said to Dennis and Ryan. "When she heads off to college next year, it'll be our loss."

"Mine, too," she lamented. "I'm going to miss eating here almost every day and seeing…everybody."

Ryan felt anyone looking at the lovestruck teen would assume that "everybody" was Adam.

Zoe turned to Ryan. "What can I get for you today?"

"Why don't you start us out with drinks and an appetizer trio tray?" Adam interjected. "I'll run down the menu so they can make informed choices."

"Great idea." Zoe pulled out a small electronic tablet and recorded their drink orders. "For the trio, how about beer balls, fried pickles and onion strings? Those are the most popular items on the starter list."

"Beer balls?" Ryan asked.

"It does sound a bit weird," Zoe replied with a laugh. "They're meatballs, made with Breedlove beef and spicy pork, then coated with a beer batter and deep-fried."

"Sounds delicious," Dennis said.

"Ryan?" Adam looked at her.

A slight hesitation and then, "That's fine."

"Are you sure?" he asked.

"Don't mind her," Dennis said. "She's one of those funny eaters…a vegetarian."

"Really?" Adam perched his Stetson on a wall hook, then reared back in his chair and observed her. "You don't eat beef or pork?"

"Nothing with a face," Ryan responded.

"Not chicken, either, or fish?"

The incredulity in his voice made Ryan laugh out loud. "None of the above."

Adam shook his head. "I'm a meat-and-potatoes man to the bone. For me, living that way would be like dying a slow and painful death." He picked up the restaurant menu, a simple two-sided sheet covered in plastic, and placed it back down with hardly a glance. "We have a couple salads on the menu," he suggested. "They're fairly straightforward but I've eaten them a time or two. Honestly, they don't get ordered much. But we wanted a few healthier options along with all the fried stuff. We also have a turkey burger but that won't help you, either."

"No, but it's okay. I'm not that hungry."

"But if you were, your choices would be limited. Honestly, with all the time we spent on the menu we didn't give vegetarians much consideration. This is a huge meat-eating town, everything with a face."

Ryan laughed. This guy was delightful.

"How long has it been since you've eaten meat?" Adam asked.

"About five years."

"Why'd you stop?"

"Because a screw came loose," Dennis joked. "Anyone who'd turn down a good burger can't be right in the head."

Adam looked at Dennis but didn't laugh. Ryan appreciated his nonresponse to her brother's barb. For as much as she loved Dennis, he could be a bully and often made her uneasy. Hurtful, disparaging comments in the guise of teasing were something she'd endured from him for much of her life.

"Do you work with your brother?" Adam asked in her silence.

Ryan glanced at Dennis. His eyes conveyed a message that she couldn't read. Her answer was noncommittal. "Not really."

"She doesn't butcher cows," Dennis said. "But she does work for me from time to time, typing and other things that can be done online. She's really good at stuff like that."

What? Updating Dennis's résumé and typing up a couple reports hardly qualified her as being Dennis's employee, especially when she did those things for free. Again Ryan assumed this was part of why she'd been brought here. To contradict him outright wouldn't look good. Dennis wouldn't like it. Ryan's mother had taught her a long time ago that Dennis was the golden child and image was everything. Even so, she barely concealed the question from being broadcast on her face.

"You live here?" Adam asked.

"Yes," Ryan answered.

Dennis turned to Ryan. "Adam works with his family but he has his own company, too, Breedlove Ranch, where they raise cows for market.

"You guys hiring?" he asked Adam. "If you have any openings in the office, Ryan here would make a great employee."

This time the message in Dennis's glance was clearly conveyed. *Play along.*

Ryan gripped her fingers together beneath the table. Otherwise she could imagine them around her brother's neck! To say that she worked with Dennis was ludicrous, and that she'd have anything to do with a company that bred animals for food was an outright lie.

But then Adam looked at her with those bedroom eyes and said, "I'm intrigued. Tell me more."

And Ryan felt that appearing to go along with her pushy brother, at least through lunch, couldn't hurt. She didn't see herself seriously dating a sexy meat-and-potatoes stallion like Adam. But she could certainly ride him for a night or two.

Two

Adam was surprised at how Dennis teased his sister, and didn't like it at all. He'd been on the receiving end of such treatment. That's how he and Dennis had become friends. The guy he remembered from high school was one who defended people who were being treated badly. That he'd been rude to his sister bothered Adam, maybe more than it should. He sensed Ryan wasn't comfortable with the situation, either. So he decided to let the matter go…for now.

Zoe returned with their drinks and to take their entrée order. Dennis and Adam opted for the house specialty and the most popular menu item—a half pound of Breedlove beef on a toasted bun topped with onion strings, dill pickle slices, and a homemade condiment blend of spicy mustard and creamy aioli.

Adam looked at Ryan. "Would you like a salad, possibly with smashed potatoes or fries?"

"What type of oil is used to cook them?" Ryan asked.

"Good question," Adam said. "I have no idea."

Ryan's query led to a visit from the chef. Once schooled in the preparation of her limited choices, her order was taken.

Dennis took a large swig of beer and then set down the bottle. "So, Adam…how'd you go from casinos to cows?"

Adam shrugged. "Wasn't planned, although if you'll remember, I always had a little bit of cowboy in me."

Dennis grinned. "That I do recall."

"Me and Christian had accompanied my father on a trip to Tokyo, where we'd just opened a second hotel. For dinner our host served us Kobe beef. It was hands down the best bite of meat I'd ever put in my mouth. I asked the host about its origins and basically became obsessed with finding out everything I could about how it was processed. When a family meeting led to a large tract of unused land being up for grabs, I jumped at the chance to come as close as I could to producing that taste in America. It's been five years in the making, but we're confident that Breedlove Ranch is about to deliver that product. Not Kobe, of course—that type can only come from the region that bears its name—but the best Wagyu beef ever produced in this country."

"Is that what's served here?" Dennis asked.

Adam shook his head. "Not yet. We've had customers sample the Wagyu, but here we'll continue to offer the less expensive prime Black Angus."

He looked over as Ryan made a face. "Sorry about that."

"No problem," Ryan responded.

"Tell that to your face," Adam drawled. "You just scrunched up your nose like you got a whiff of poo."

The comment caused Ryan to burst out laughing yet again. From a woman who Adam felt was somewhat guarded, the sound was as carefree as it was unexpected. It was a sound he decided he quite liked. A lot.

"Where is your meat processed?" Dennis asked.

Adam glanced at Ryan before answering. "Until now we've sold the bulk of cattle wholesale, keeping back a supply for the hotel, a few restaurants and stores in this area, that are processed by a small, family-owned business in Henderson. But we're four to eight weeks away from completing our own facility."

"Having your own processing plant has got to be exciting."

"It is," Adam replied. "Four thousand square feet, state of the art."

Adam saw Ryan reach for her purse. "Excuse me," she said, standing up.

"Don't go," Adam responded. "We can talk shop another time."

"No, really. It's okay. I want to wash my hands."

Adam watched her walk away. He was struck by her beauty to be sure—curvy figure, curly hair, skin the color of hot cocoa and he imagined just as sweet. But there was something else about her, an aura of calm assuredness, a peacefulness that somehow calmed him, too. These days, as he balanced his responsibilities at CANN International with the expanded growth and heightening profile of Breedlove Ranch and the beef it produced, moments of true tranquility were in short supply.

"I see you," Dennis said with a smile in his voice. "Checking out my sister."

Until then Adam didn't realize he'd been staring. "I

never knew you had a sister. I remember your brother Charles, but not her."

"Everyone thought Charles and I were brothers. He's my cousin."

"You're right, I didn't know that. We became close rather quickly in high school but you were a senior when we met. It was only that one year."

"Makes sense about Ryan," Dennis replied. "That you never met her. She was several years behind us in school and I don't think you ever came to my home."

"That's because you guys were always wanting to come over to mine!"

"Heck, yeah. Who wouldn't? Swimming pools. Horses. A full basketball court. Dinners made to order from a personal chef. Going to your house was like going to Hollywood! I couldn't believe people really lived like that. You're one lucky dude."

"I'll admit to luck in being born a Breedlove. After that, everything was hard work."

"I know all about hard work," Dennis said.

"At the meatpacking plant, right?" Dennis nodded. "How does Ryan fit into your operation?"

Adam ignored Dennis's knowing smile, one that suggested the sister had been brought along to help seal the deal. It was a good move and a smart one, but Adam figured Dennis didn't have to know that.

"Like I said, she's helped out here and there. But she doesn't live in Bakersfield, hasn't in a while. She went to school in San Diego and lived there after graduation. Until about three months ago when she moved here."

"Why'd she move?"

Dennis shrugged. "She got a degree in some kind of natural medicine or something. I don't know much about it. But I know she isn't working anywhere yet. She probably needs a job."

"And you think she'd be comfortable working on a ranch?"

Ryan returned to the table. "Talking about me?"

Adam stood but he was too late. Ryan had already pulled out her chair. He waited until she'd sat down before returning to his seat.

"Dennis thinks you'd be a good fit for my operation. He says your administrative skills are impressive."

And if they are half as impressive as the view of your backside as you walked away from the table...

Adam shut down the inappropriate thought, gave himself a mental chastisement, forgave himself because his thought was the truth, then refocused his attention on Ryan.

"I handled a few items for him in the past, but that was a long time ago. I'm focused on developing my own business right now."

"Which is?"

"Naturopathy," Ryan said after a pause.

"What's that?" Adam asked as he watched Ryan stiffen as though expecting a verbal blow. Dennis didn't disappoint.

"A hobby," Dennis said.

"My career," Ryan countered, a cool breeze skittering over the previously warm and calm demeanor Adam had earlier observed.

"Lunch is served!" Zoe announced as she arrived at their table, moving a few items before expertly setting down a circular tray. "Both the pickles and onion strings are vegan," she said to Ryan, having obviously spoken with the chef. "The barbecue sauce is also vegan but the buttermilk ranch contains dairy. Your entrées will be up in about ten minutes. Bon appétit!"

"These are cool," Ryan said, using the tongs hooked to the bowl to pull out a wad of thinly cut and battered onion slices. "Onion strings, huh? I've had onion rings and a flowering onion but never ones quite like this."

"That's Miguel's handiwork. He puts a unique spin on any dish he touches."

"I like the beer balls," Dennis said around the food he'd picked up with his fingers and plopped into his mouth. "That big old juicy burger will be even better. Good old cow meat," he continued, smacking loudly and reaching for another meatball.

"Older brothers can be a pain in the butt," he said to Ryan. "I know, I've got one, too."

Ryan smiled. Adam immediately wanted to think of something else witty to make her smile again.

"Good to know someone else understands my pain."

"He's not all bad, though," Adam continued. "Standing up to bullies is how I met your brother."

"You mean he wasn't one of them?"

Adam laughed. "Not that time."

"What happened?" Ryan asked.

Adam and Dennis exchanged a look.

Adam thought back to the day as a freshman in high school where he had fought an admirable but losing battle against four students who'd ganged up against him—at first verbally, then physically. Dennis had come to Adam's defense. The two had quickly regained the upper hand before school administrators rushed into the melee and broke up the fight. It was Adam's last physical fight. That summer his muscles filled out and he grew six inches. Once his dyslexia was properly diagnosed, his popularity grew along with his confidence.

But still, scars remained. There were traces of the disability that lingered to this day.

"Kids were always teasing me. One day, I found myself in a fight where I was outnumbered," Adam said. "Your brother jumped in and helped me out. That's how we became friends."

"Interesting," Ryan said, giving her brother a look that Adam couldn't quite read.

"I always appreciated how you took up for me," Adam finished. "Just like one of my brothers would, had they been there. It showed character, which is very important to me. That along with loyalty, honesty and respect are the principle virtues I look for in people I work with. Which is why I wanted to have lunch with you today, Dennis. You mentioned your sister working for me but actually the opening I'm trying to fill ASAP requires a different skill set. The person we'd hired to manage my processing facility was involved in a serious automobile accident. He's alive, but his recovery isn't going to allow for the type of rigor required for that position. Are you interested?"

Dennis sat back. "Wow, really, Adam? You're offering me the job of managing your meat-processing operation?"

"I'm asking if you're interested. We'd still need to go through the application process, but if everything from there is in order then yes, I'd feel good in you having that job."

"Thanks, man. I appreciate it and yes, I'm very interested. I've always loved your family's land. Working on it would be my pleasure."

"I might come up to Bakersfield," Adam said. "Get a look at your operation and see how it compares to ours."

"Okay," Dennis said, after a beat.

Adam found the hesitation odd but didn't dwell on it. Now that he'd potentially solved a huge dilemma, a delay that would have put a serious wrench in their scheduled plant launch, he was ready to find out more about Ryan. Whether or not he ended up working with Dennis, he wanted to see more of her. Before parting ways he asked Dennis to send him a proposal, and asked Ryan for her number.

"Why?" Ryan asked, her expression suggesting she couldn't think of a reason why he'd need to talk to her.

Adam smiled slightly, impressed. Most women were all too eager to give him their number. He was appreciative of one who hesitated. "To talk about food," he replied, "and what types of vegetarian options might work with our current menu."

She seemed relieved that his reason was work related. It wasn't the only one, of course, but it was as good of an excuse as any.

Three

Ryan hadn't been surprised yesterday when Dennis ran off before she could confront him. He hadn't returned her calls from last night or yesterday, either. Blindsiding her with a job she'd never heard of in front of the man wanting to hire him was pretty low, even for a brother known for sometimes being underhanded. But honestly, Ryan couldn't be totally mad. Adam Breedlove was one hot man. She had no intention of working at Breedlove Ranch but she could put in a personal shift or two with the boss. She'd been in the city for three months without dating. One day after the other had been all work, no play. Dennis's friend could prove a nice lightweight diversion. A little sin in Sin City every now and again.

The prospect of a rendezvous with the cowboy was totally titillating, but Ryan forced her mind back to where it belonged this Monday morning—on her practice, and building it up. After years of sharing "her hobby" as Dennis had called it with friends, classmates and coworkers, she'd gotten serious about her love for alternative healing and obtained a bachelor's degree in naturopathy, specializing in plant medicine, biophysics, massage therapy and nutrition. She'd simultaneously pursued and received certificates in energetic healing and emotional frequency technique from the prestigious Institute of Higher Holistic Learning in La Jolla, California. From her childhood until her early-adult years as she came into her own, she'd sought to please others and be what they thought she should be. After learning of her passion, her parents had suggested traditional medicine, had thought she should pursue a nursing degree. But Ryan had finally followed her heart and become submerged in Eastern medicine and alternative forms of healing. Those three years of expedited learning were the best ones of her life. This was also when she'd met her ex, which had added some worst moments to those educational years.

While attending an expo during her senior year she'd met Brooklyn, a woman named for where she'd been born, who'd moved cross-country to Las Vegas, a place Ryan had doubted she'd ever return to live. But their long conversations on the alternative and holistic landscape evolved into others on working in complementary fields. Their shared interests and similar personalities led to them being best friends, the sister Ryan had always wanted. Brooklyn suggested they open a practice together. Ryan jumped at the chance to have her own business. That's why she'd moved back to Las Vegas. Not the only one, but the one she felt most comfortable admitting. The other reasons were complicated, both hopeful and painful. There were secrets she hadn't unearthed and couldn't share...yet.

Ryan's ringing landline startled her out of daydreaming. A blessed interruption, she inwardly noted, while crossing the airy living room of her Summerlin townhome. No doubt it was Brooklyn, calling to make sure Ryan was on schedule and that she'd make it to their appointment on time.

"Yes, I'm ready. Five minutes and I'm out the door."

"Um, okay, but where are we going?"

Ryan's heart raced. "Adam?"

He chuckled, a sound that sent goose bumps dancing over her skin.

"I hope it's okay that Dennis gave me your home number. I tried your cell phone a couple times but didn't hear back, and the question I have is time-sensitive so I called your brother."

Halfway through his explanation, Ryan had begun searching for her cell. She'd checked the living room and master bedroom. Now she headed toward the garage.

"Ryan, are you there? If this is a bad time—"

"No, it isn't," Ryan said, while lying on her belly and searching her car's back seat. "I'm looking for my cell phone that I now realize I haven't heard ring all morning."

"When is the last time you remember having it?"

"Definitely this morning before leaving the house. I tried calling Dennis in fact and…aw!"

"Whoa, are you okay?"

"Yes!" Ryan laughed. "I just remembered where it was." She headed into her house and the bedroom. "I forgot I placed it in my yoga bag before going into the studio."

She found the bag in her closet, opened it up and

retrieved the phone. "Listen, Adam, if you're calling about what Dennis is doing—"

"I'm not."

"Oh." Ryan glanced at the clock on the wall. It was almost time to head out for her meeting. But she had five minutes. She sat down. Adam's voice was better than a massage. It made her feel all noodly, if that was even a word.

"What's up?"

"Magic, if you're into that sort of thing."

If you're doing the tricks, I very well could be. "What kind of magic?"

"What kind do you like?"

His voice had lowered just enough for Ryan to imagine a double entendre. If his bedroom moves were half as sexy as that raspy tenor…

"All kinds, I guess. I find fantasy entertaining. The ability to conjure another type of world within this one is an incredible skill."

"I agree. Our hotel is hosting a private premiere that we feel is going to be very special. It is a show that blends illusion with dance, great music and scenes. Rather than separate tricks, an entire story is told. The guy is from Denmark. His name is Valdemar."

"Never heard of him."

"Few have, in America. At least not yet. And no one in the way he'll be presented at CANN. The show is tomorrow night and I'd like very much for you to join me."

"It sounds interesting. What time?" Ryan asked, as though it mattered. Mentally, she was already going through her closet for what to wear, but a girl couldn't appear too hasty.

"The show starts at nine but I was hoping you'd also join me for dinner. I spoke with hotel management, who recommended a couple of our restaurants with stellar vegan and vegetarian choices."

"That's very thoughtful of you." *Or presumptive.*

"I wanted to be prepared, just in case you said yes." Ryan hesitated.

"I know it's late notice. I wasn't planning to go until, well, I caught a bit of the rehearsal and what I saw blew me away."

"It sounds incredible, Adam. I'd love to join you."

"May I pick you up around…six thirty?"

"Are you sure? I could meet you there."

"No way. I'll come to you. What's your address?"

Ryan rattled off her address while gathering her tablet and a couple folders and placing them in a stylish hemp tote. She ended the call, exchanged house shoes for a pair of wooden throwback clogs that she adored, placed her clutch inside the tote and walked to the car with her cell phone in hand. There was one more call she needed to make.

As soon as her Bluetooth engaged, Ryan called Dennis, at the office this time. "I need to speak to my brother, Katy. I know he's there so tell him to pick up or I'm coming over."

"Um, Dennis isn't here," Katy said.

"You sound uncertain. Are you sure?"

"Let me check and call you back."

"I've been waiting for callbacks, Katy. I hate to put you in the middle of this, but I really need to talk to Dennis, now."

"I'll find him for you and either he'll call back or I will, promise."

Ten minutes later, her phone rang.

"Hey, sis!"

"Don't 'sis' me. You owe me an explanation regarding lunch this weekend. What was that about?"

"What do you mean?"

"You know full well what I mean. I never worked for you, have zero interest in being a secretary and am not looking for a job. Of course you don't know this because you never asked me. We haven't talked in weeks."

"Ah, Ryan, don't be upset. I could tell Adam liked you and played on it is all, hoping his interest in you would give me an advantage when I asked him for a job. Turns out that didn't happen because he asked me!"

Ryan sighed. "I'm glad it worked out for you, Dennis. But from here on out, don't put me in the middle of your business, okay?"

"That's fair, sis. I just have one more request."

"What?"

"You're coming home next week, right?"

"How do you know about that?"

"Mom told me."

"Yes, I'm going home. Why?"

"Adam wants to visit my, um, facility and I thought it would be cool if I schedule his visit at the same time you're here so we can all have dinner together."

"What'd I just say about involving me in your meat-factory business? I don't want to take part in it."

"I know, and after this, you won't. It's just that Adam is big on family, huge. Mom likes that and wants to have him over for dinner. Your being here could be a buffer. Mom isn't always the most gracious person, you know."

"Yes, I know." She had a son who was just like her.

Ryan reached the block where her business rental was located. She pulled into the parking lot, found a space and parked.

"I get a feeling there's more to this. What aren't you telling me?"

"That's it, I swear! Mom says you'll be here Friday. I'll ask Adam to come up then, and Mom will do dinner that night. Cool?" Ryan's eyes narrowed as she tried to get a feel for what was really going on.

"It's all about family, Ryan. I'm asking you to help me the way we've helped you, all right?"

Of course he'd pull that card. "I guess, but after this I'm out. Are we clear?"

Dennis laughed. "Don't get all huffy just because you've got a billionaire interested in you. I could tell him a few things to make him change his mind."

Ryan ended the call more conflicted than ever. Going on the date with Adam now felt like a bad idea. She found him super good-looking and was madly attracted, but did she really want to go on a date and maybe sleep with a guy that her brother might end up working with? Someone she might have to see after a fling?

No, she didn't. She couldn't, especially now, just as she was about to open her business. Few people knew what Dennis threatened to share with Adam, details of a painful past she'd worked hard to overcome. One that for twenty years her adoptive mother, Ida, had encouraged her to keep secret. She'd demanded that her "embarrassing" birth mother, Phyllis, be left in the past. That Ryan had been in contact with Phyllis off and on for the past five years would definitely anger her. As would the latest secret, that for the first time in Ryan's life, she was going to try and find her birth father.

Dennis was right. There were things Adam didn't know, facts hidden beneath a carefully crafted facade of perfectly placed secrets. Even without her dysfunctional history, a man like Adam was clearly out of her league. For a while, though, she'd forgotten, had allowed herself to believe that she could have the fairy-tale life of her childhood dreams. Happily-ever-after came only in books, something Ryan would do well to remember.

Four

Adam strolled out of the hotel's private entrance, eased into the roomy back seat of the car that awaited and clipped the hanger holding his suit jacket over the bar. He hoped Ryan wouldn't consider his transportation choice bougie, although that was a fairly apt description for an executive limousine. Any other woman and he wouldn't have given it a second thought, knew that picking up most dates in the company's brand-new four-seater SUV limo would impress them right out of their undies. Not that he was thinking about Ryan's lingerie. He'd be lying to say that since meeting her such thoughts hadn't crossed his mind from time to time.

Ryan lived in Summerlin, just over ten miles from the Strip. Adam thought of a few things he could do in the twenty-five or so minutes it would take to reach her, longer if traffic didn't cooperate. There were emails to answer, phone calls to return. But instead of returning calls or checking texts or browsing emails he dropped his head, closed his eyes and thought about how Ryan had tried to get out of attending the show with him tonight. He couldn't remember ever having a woman try to break a date. Why had Ryan? And for a man who could go out with just about anyone he wanted, especially when only interested in a casual good time, maybe a bedroom rodeo, why had her canceling their date not been an option?

"Something came up," she'd said. He'd told her she couldn't cancel. When asked why he'd calmly replied, "This is a major event with huge implications for the continued success of this particular hotel venue. Every RSVP has already been tabulated into the report for our board. I can't show up alone and there is no time to call in a replacement. You've given your word. I'll be there in an hour." Five minutes later, he'd walked to the car.

What Ryan didn't know was that what Breedloves wanted, Breedloves got. Period, point-blank, end of story.

They pulled into one of Summerlin's planned communities and onto a street ending in a cul-de-sac framed by townhome-styled condos. One had a red door with earthen pots on each side, brimming with flowers and greenery.

"A hundred bucks that's Ryan's home," he said to the driver, who checked the address and nodded at Adam.

"Good thing I didn't take you up on that bet."

Adam got out of the car and strolled up to the door. A burst of excitement spread from his core to his groin. With a smorgasbord of women to choose from any given night of the week, he'd grown jaded to the art of wining and dining. It felt good to be excited. He rang the bell.

"Un momento," she sang out. *Gringo Spanish.* He thought about Miguel and smiled.

In less than a minute, she opened the door. Adam turned, but wasn't ready for the woman he saw. Not this Ryan—part innocent femininity, part femme fatale. The dress, long and flowing, following her curves like water followed the falls. The color almost matched her tawny skin, making him imagine her nude. At the restaurant her curls had been tamed by a band on top of her head but tonight they bounced wild and free, framing her face and brushing her shoulders. They teased his senses; he wanted to touch. He liked that she wore little makeup yet still looked flawless. Her lips kissed with a color of gloss that reminded him of a fine wine. He wanted a taste. How was it that with most of her body covered she managed to look so sexy?

"Hello" was all he said at first because it was all he could manage.

"Hi."

"I'm sorry for earlier, and sounding so forceful. It's just that I couldn't take no for an answer."

"It's okay. Everything…worked out." Ryan turned and locked the door. Adam offered his arm. Her touch was light, yet a thunderbolt of desire shot through his heart, ricocheted off a vein and zoomed into his groin.

He helped her enter the vehicle, then got in on the other side.

"You look…stunning."

The smile that she gave him could have cured a disease. "I hoped it would be appropriate. I wasn't sure."

"It's perfect."

"Thank you."

Adam's brow furrowed. "Are you sure you're okay?"

"It's just that… Yes. Really, I'm fine."

The SUV pulled away from the curb. Ryan took in the roomy interior. "This is nice."

She sat perched on the seat, taking in the swank decor. "I've never been in something like this before. From the outside it looked like an SUV but in here…"

He watched as she ran her hand across the lambskin seat. Her eyes, initially reticent, now sparkled while examining the console, with its built-in bottle chiller, various openers and glass rack. She stopped suddenly, as if becoming aware of her innocent wonder. She may have thought he'd find it amusing. He thought it endearing, and with a trail of showgirls, sycophants and rich chicks in his wake, a breath of fresh air.

"So this is a limo?"

He nodded. "It's called an executive SUV."

"I like it."

A brow raised. "You don't mind that it has leather seats?"

"I'm not a member of the PETA police, Adam, you can relax."

He made a big show of taking a breath, which made her laugh as he'd intended.

"While I don't own a gun or a hunting license, my choice to be vegetarian is for nutritional reasons, mostly. I am cognizant of the earth's precarious state and do what I can to try to protect the planet. I believe our bodies are our temples so I make an effort to be kind to mine. But I try not to be a holistic zealot trying to win everyone over to my point of view.

"That said…" She paused dramatically. "There are faux materials that work just as well or even better than cowhide, and mushroom dishes that would make you throw away your steak."

"Baby," Adam drawled, "unless that mushroom had

hooves and could moo, trust me, there'd be no competition."

She was funny and natural and easy to talk to, yet emanated a vulnerability that brought out his chivalrous side. He wanted to protect her. From what, he had no idea. By the time they'd rounded back to the hotel, the stress of Adam's day had faded, the questions he'd had about her demeanor forgotten for now.

They entered the hotel through the private entrance and once inside the elevator, Adam accessed the panel to bypass all floors and take them straight to Zest, CANN Casino Hotel and Spa's premier restaurant, located on the building's one hundredth floor. As the elevator zoomed to the top, Ryan stepped closer to Adam and gripped his arm.

"Afraid of heights?"

"No, but I'm not fond of rockets masquerading as elevators."

"I've got you, girl." He placed an arm around her, grateful for a reason to brush a hand across her soft skin. "Stay close to me and don't worry about a thing."

The elevator doors opened, and as the host led them around the corner, Adam was rewarded with the gasp of awe that escaped every newcomer's lips to the wonder that was the hotel's crowning architectural and culinary masterpiece. With exquisite attention to detail, the main dining room, with a seating capacity for 140 guests, still afforded many booths semiprivacy, space between tables and an unobstructed view of the world beyond through floor-to-ceiling paneless windows that brought the outdoors inside. Classical music delicately played provided a subtle melody for the low murmur of conversation heard as Adam and Ryan were led to a booth. Its back created a wall between them and the other guests, while before them lay the whole of the Vegas Strip.

"Do you want to go for a closer look?"

Ryan shook her head as he finished the question. "It's the most phenomenal view of this city I've ever seen, but believe me, I'm good."

They sat down to a table set with linen and china, a bottle of sparkling water cooling on ice.

"This is so pretty," Ryan said wistfully. "To think that this is everyday life for some people is a bit unbelievable. I feel like Cinderella."

"Does that mean I'm your prince?"

"Until the clock strikes midnight," Ryan said, her voice low as her eyes sparkled with seduction. Then, in an instant, the vulnerability reappeared. "Then I'll have to run away before the carriage becomes a pumpkin and my clothes turn back to rags."

"Have I told you how much I like rags?" Asked so earnestly that not only did Ryan laugh but Adam cracked himself up as well. "In fact I think I'm going to start a clothing line. Rags by Adam."

"All cotton, no leather," Ryan teased.

"Not cotton," Adam responded, "leaves."

Adam loved to hear Ryan laugh. While far from being a comedian, he'd turned the mood funny so that a certain body part straining to stand at attention would return to its at-ease position. The next few minutes was a parade of perfection as the sommelier, the maître d' and their personal server ensured them the best of dining experiences.

After toasting to the belief in magic, the two newfound friends settled against their seats and looked at each other, comfortable in the silence, each in their own thoughts of what the night was and all it could become.

Ryan cocked her head. "What?"

"You don't like me looking at you?"

"Worse could happen. But you're frowning."

"I guess I'm trying to figure you out. You're as different from Dennis as night is from day. I only met your dad a time or two but I remember him as a quiet man. I'd say you were more like him."

"I can be quiet," Ryan replied. "I guess we have that in common."

"So Dennis must be more like your mom."

"They are almost exactly alike."

"It will be good to see them again after all these years. And you'll be there, too, Dennis says."

Ryan nodded.

"Do you get back often to visit?"

"A few times a year, holidays mostly. But since my dad's diagnosis, I've tried to go more frequently, and with the business about to open I thought that now, before that happened, would be a good time."

"What's going on with your father, if you don't mind me asking?"

"He has chronic kidney disease."

"I'm so sorry."

"Me, too."

"How long has he had it?"

"Apparently much longer than anyone realized. He battled diabetes and high blood pressure for years. No one knew how much havoc was being wreaked on his kidneys. The symptoms were always attributed to what we already knew."

Adam observed the hurt reflected in Ryan's face as she nervously bit her lip. Clearly, she loved her father. For a Breedlove, that kind of family devotion was a very endearing trait.

"Is that what made you want to study…"

"Naturopathy? That was part of it. But I've always had compassion for anyone hurting. I watched people struggle and wanted to help them, especially as a little girl."

Adam watched as another flicker of pain flitted across her face. He wondered who caused it even as he felt an urge to protect her from it ever happening again.

"My parents thought I'd be a nurse. But I can't stand the sight of blood, which in the field of nursing is a bit problematic."

"Then you'd definitely not fare well at a meat-processing plant."

"Definitely not. During my senior year of high school I went to a job fair and discovered alternative-based medicine. It's where I first heard the word *naturopathy*. Before the hour was over I knew what I wanted to do. Now, I'm here."

"About to open your own business?"

"Yes. Me and a partner are opening our own practice in a strip mall not far from here."

"What services will you offer?"

"My specialties include whole food nutrition, that's a plant-centered diet, and energy healing that includes therapeutic massage."

"Hmm." Adam's eyes brightened. "I've got a few kinks. Can you work them out?"

"Kinks I can get rid of, but your eyes are sending a more kinky vibe. I'm not sure I can take care of that."

"But you could try." He reached for Ryan's hand. It was soft and delicate, engulfed in his much larger one. Her nails were manicured and squared. She wore no rings. "Yes, I think you should try. These feel like magic hands."

"They're healing hands," Ryan corrected, slowly pulling her hand out of his while looking in his eyes.

It was as though Adam felt every cell on her delicate skin. He wanted the time to touch more of it, all of it, everywhere. "For someone who's sick, healing is magical. And I get the feeling that for any number of ailments that I might encounter, your...magic...could be the cure."

The teasing continued, flirting increased and lust heightened through six incredible courses. Just as they finished up a decadent concoction of sweetness that gave dates, coconut, gelato and cacao nibs new meaning, Adam checked his watch. The timing was perfect. The show was set to begin in the Jewel, a two-thousand-seat state-of-the-art arena named for Adam's grandmother. Between the two of them a bottle of Krug had disappeared. Alcohol always stirred Adam's libido and it appeared to stoke Ryan's fire as well.

The arm that held Ryan's slid to her waist as they neared the elevator. She wasn't petite exactly, and her body felt toned, but her five foot five was overshadowed by his six foot two, even with her sexy stilettos. He felt protective and probably wouldn't have been able to keep his hands off her even if he hadn't remembered her aversion to the fast-moving car.

"Are you ready for magic?" he asked as they descended.

She turned to him, her eyes sincere. "I thought it had already begun."

Adam squeezed her waist gently and then dropped his hand. It wasn't Ryan's fault that she'd lit him up like a match soaked in gasoline. His body was burning with desire. He hoped in time the enchanter beside him could help douse the flame.

Five

Her birthday wasn't for another two weeks, but Ryan knew that no celebration she could dream up or afford would top what was happening tonight. Since this was the only date she'd have with Adam, she intended to make the most of it. The champagne helped her push thoughts of possible repercussions or regrets to the back of her mind. As they ascended the stairs to enter the Jewel arena, she was aware of both admiring and envious eyes. Adam cut a suave figure as he walked next to her in a suit tailored to the perfection of his lean frame. The finely spun black wool matched his close-cropped curls, soft, she knew, because her hand had brushed across them in the elevator when she'd picked an imaginary piece of lint from his suit jacket collar, just to be able to touch them. The white shirt he'd paired it with emphasized his bronze skin and dark brown eyes. He walked with assurance and purpose, seemingly comfortable with all of the attention afforded him. For Ryan, this was a whole new world, one in which she wondered if she could ever be comfortable. Adam had called her beautiful but her dress, as much as she liked it and as pretty as it was, paled in comparison to the diamonds, beaded gowns and designer everything that surrounded her. She saw more than one woman sweep her from head to toe and decide she was hardly worthy of Adam's attention, much less his arm. The devil on her shoulder told her they were right. She tried to ignore them by going within as Brooklyn would tell her, to summon an inner angel to counter those negative voices with the truth, that she was enough, just the way she was.

It also helped still feelings of inadequacy by looking past judgmental faces and focusing on the elaborate entryway. It was, in a word, magnificent, and the interior, too. She thought it impossible for any space to outdo Zest but that feat had been accomplished. When it came to glitz and glam, Las Vegas was known for its gaudy, sometimes garish displays. But in this room the theme of jewels was understated and sophisticated. The ceiling twinkled with them, like stars in the sky, a 3-D effect allowing one to believe they could reach out and touch them, while in actuality they were more than thirty feet away. They reached a center aisle dividing the orchestra section from the lower tier. Adam led them down that center aisle toward a curtained entry.

"I probably should have warned you sooner," he said softly as they passed through the curtain and mounted a short flight of stairs. "But you're about to meet my parents."

She stopped their movement. "What?"

"They won't bite you," he said, and the dazzling smile he shared with her chased the initial panic away.

"But just so you know, my mom's a matchmaker who'll try to learn your life between acts. You're under no obligation to allow her to pry, or to answer questions, no matter how skillful her attempted extraction. Are we good?"

"I guess so," she responded. They continued around the corner and up another short flight. "Though had I known I was going to be meeting your family I may not have drunk that last glass of champagne."

"Don't worry, Ryan Washington. Just be yourself."

They entered a private box to the right of the aisle. It contained ten chairs, of which six were occupied. A beautiful couple sat in the two front left chairs. They turned and smiled. At once Ryan knew they were Adam's parents. He had his dad's eyes and his mother's smile. There was another couple beside them of similar age and a handsome young man behind them stamped with the Breedlove beauty that the girl beside him clearly adored. She took in this tableau within the seconds it took to cross the wide aisle and enter the booth.

Both older men stood. "Mr. Chapman!" Adam returned the middle-aged gentleman's hearty greeting and kissed the hand of the woman smiling at them from her seat. "Sherry, you look lovely as always.

"Greg, Sherry, this is Ryan Washington. Ryan, the Chapmans. Greg works at CANN and both are longtime friends."

Ryan shook their hands. "It's a pleasure to meet both of you. Sherry, I love your necklace."

"I was just going to say the same about yours. I've never seen a design quite like it. So…bohemian chic!"

Ryan's hand went to the chakra necklace she'd purchased during a visit to Taos, New Mexico. Made with crystals ranging from amethyst to yellow topaz to trapiche emeralds, the jewelry had cost a small fortune, a graduation present to herself. "It's one of my favorite pieces."

"Dear, you wear it very well."

They continued to where the woman Ryan assumed was Adam's mother stood with his father, a thought that was confirmed when he gave both a warm embrace.

"About time you got here," the man said. "The doors will lock once the show starts and this is one you don't want to miss."

"We were here," Adam responded. "Just finishing dinner at Zest."

Ryan noted a suddenly raised brow above the kind eyes that viewed her. "You had dinner at Zest?" she asked. She looked from Adam to Ryan. "The lovely woman on your arm must be special indeed!"

"Ryan had never been there," Adam answered. "Mom, Dad, this is Ryan Washington. She's Dennis Washington's sister. Remember the guy who used to beg for Gabe's cinnamon rolls every time he came to the house?"

"The young man who that one summer practically lived in our pool?" Mrs. Breedlove asked.

"That was Dennis," Adam responded with a laugh. "Ryan, these are two of the greatest parents in the world, my mom, Victoria, and my dad, Nicholas."

Victoria stepped forward and pulled Ryan into a light embrace. "It's wonderful to meet you, Ryan. You look lovely tonight."

"It is my pleasure," Ryan responded. "I'm looking forward to the show."

She offered a hand to Adam's father but he brushed it away. "Handshakes are for business deals," he said, giving her shoulders an affectionate squeeze. "Hugs are for friends of the family."

"It's nice to meet you, Mr. Breedlove."

"Please, call me Nicholas."

"Okay, Nicholas. Thank you."

"And I'm Victoria."

"All right."

"Had I known you were bringing a guest," Victoria said to Adam, "I would have rearranged the seating. It would have been great for your date and me to get to know each other better."

"Exactly what I was afraid of," Adam retorted, which earned him a frown from Ryan, a laugh from Nicholas and a slap on his forearm from Victoria. "Looks like the show will be starting soon. We'd better take our seats."

After a quick introduction to one of Adam's younger brothers, Noah, and his date, the two settled into comfortable, spacious seating where Ryan proceeded to be mesmerized by the best and most beautiful show she'd ever seen in her life. Valdemar was more than a magician; he was a creative genius who transported the audience to imaginary worlds.

A magnificently performed trick left Adam's eyes bright with wonder, and Ryan even more thrilled to have been invited, to be the woman sitting beside him enjoying the show. When in the finale everything on the stage seemed to disappear, Ryan joined Adam and everyone around her in an enthusiastic standing ovation. The handsome Valdemar had almost convinced her that magic was real and dreams did come true. Ryan allowed herself to enjoy the moment but knew from experience that magic was for arenas like this and dreams were for sleeping. No matter how beautiful, eventually one woke up and the dream came to an end.

"Was that not the most spectacular show ever?" Victoria beamed, squeezing Ryan's hands in her own.

"I'm speechless," Ryan responded. "I've never seen anything like it."

Victoria turned to Adam. "Are you two joining us backstage? There's going to be a brief meet and greet and reception for the cast and special guests."

Ryan looked at Adam. She could have drowned in the depth of desire she saw in his eyes. They'd rarely spoken throughout the magical performance but she knew he'd felt the energy emanating from the stage as deeply as she, and was fully prepared for him to turn down his mother's invitation for a romp in the nearest hotel suite.

Instead he placed an arm around Ryan. "Would you like to meet Valdemar?"

"Of course."

He looked at his parents. "After you," he said.

Valdemar was as quietly introspective in person as he was gregarious and commanding onstage. They met other people, too, familiar faces Ryan had seen on television or in magazines. People were gracious, but Ryan couldn't help feeling that she didn't belong. She was glad when they left the Jewel and arrived at the car, where the driver stood at an open door. Happy that the trek through the hotel was over, Ryan climbed inside. Once seated, she immediately leaned forward and removed her shoes.

"Oh my goodness, my feet are killing me!"

Adam settled in beside her. "May I?"

Desire, already pooled at the base of her core, splashed and bubbled over, sprinkling her feminine flower with dew. "Sure."

He hit a button. The privacy partition raised. His eyes bored into hers as he pulled her feet into his lap and ran a large hand over the sole of her foot. His gaze dropped then as strong, sure fingers began massaging her heel, pressing against the ball of her foot and caressing her toes one by one.

"Am I doing it correctly?" he asked.

Ryan closed her eyes and leaned into the limo's cushiness. "That feels so good."

He finished one foot and reached for the other. Ryan was vaguely aware that music had been turned on, barely recognizable because so was she! Who cared that he was out of her orbit? At the moment she wanted nothing more than for this man, Adam Breedlove, to make hot and passionate love to her, to send her to another world. Would he think her too easy if she asked for what she wanted, nothing deep or serious, but a night filled with mind-blowing pleasure, the kind she would have bet money that Adam could provide? He was Dennis's friend, something that would have normally been problematic, except one, she'd never been attracted to any of his other friends, and two, what happened between her and Adam was something that Dennis didn't need to know. She and Adam had flirted all evening. Had he been dropping real hints about how he wanted the evening to end, or just testing the waters? When she felt his fingers leave her heel and proceed up her ankle and gently squeeze her shin, she threw caution to the wind and decided to find out.

She lowered her foot so that it touched his leg, slowly ran it up his muscled thigh until it rested near his crotch. Her eyes flittered open to find his narrowing as he sucked in a breath. It was all the encouragement she needed. That single simple intake of air unleashed a torrent of physical craving from inside her, brought out a boldness not normally possessed. She brought her feet to the floor and shifted her body closer to him, placed a hand on his chest and leaned in.

"May I?" she asked in a whisper, catching his answer with her lips.

Adam responded by opening his mouth and swiping his tongue in a manner that suggested that she do the same. She did; their tongues touched and danced and mimicked each other, even as she felt Adam's arm slide around to her waist and down to her butt. Having expected a kiss that was hard and demanding, as powerful as Adam's long-legged strides, she was surprised at the softness with which he approached her, how he nibbled her lower lip and kissed her cheek before sliding his tongue back into her mouth. He kissed her slowly, thoroughly, as if savoring the taste of her. His leisurely kiss, deep and hot, drove Ryan crazy. She moved closer, her hands finally able to play in the curls the way she wanted before sliding down and over broad shoulders and back to the nape of his neck. Adam's hands moved in time with hers, one sliding beneath the silky fabric of her dress and tickling her thighs. She moaned, her hips moving of their own accord, to a rhythm she wanted to dance with the partner beside her. Then something happened.

The car stopped.

Ryan opened her eyes and took in the red door of her condo, softly lit by the porch light she'd turned on when they left.

"We're here already?" She sat back, straightening her dress. "That was fast."

"Too fast," Adam said.

She looked into his eyes, wondering if she should voice her desire. With this next question there'd be no turning back.

"Would you like to come inside?"

Adam's smile was slight as he shook his head. "No. I want to go home."

Her heart fell. A man like Adam? She should have known. She gathered her purse and made a move for the door.

Strong fingers clamped around her arm, holding her fast. "Wait! I want you to come with me so that we can...finish what we've started. Would you like that?"

Ryan laid her head on his shoulder. "I'd love that."

She watched Adam push a button and tell the driver, "Elvis, change of plans. Take me home."

Ryan closed her eyes as she felt Adam's lips against her temple, his hand stroking her hair. Those blasted whispers tried to push through the haze of happiness and warn her that she was just being used and would then be tossed away. She shut her mind and refused to listen. She was a twenty-first-century woman who knew what she wanted. If in fact Adam was using her, so be it. Because tonight she planned to put his hard, strong body to good use, too.

Six

Adam relished the feel of Ryan in his arms. They needed to talk before…whatever…to establish what this night was and, more important, what it was not. He'd faced uncomfortable situations more than once when a woman's inability to remain emotionally detached had turned one night of pleasure into months of pain. There were those who had ulterior motives, who'd used various means to try to trap him or begin a relationship with him as a way to increase their social status or bank account. He could spot women like that a mile away before he turned twenty-one, thanks in large part to a caring older brother who used his own experiences as lessons for Adam. He'd had his own teachers, too, and the hard knocks as proof. He didn't feel any of that energy coming from Ryan. From her, all he felt was sensual heat.

But they still needed to talk.

"I'm really feeling you, beautiful," he began, pulling

his arms more tightly around her. "But we need to make sure we're on the same page so that later there will be no hurt feelings or misunderstandings."

Ryan sat up and away from him. "Well, that's a first."

"What?"

"A man trying to kick me out of his bed before I ever get in it."

Adam groaned. "That's not it at all." He tried to pull Ryan back into him but she resisted.

"I'm teasing, but I get it. Before we get all caught up in the throes of passion you're wanting to make sure I'm not some crazy stalker type who will see tonight as anything more than it is—two mutually consenting adults coming together to give each other what we both want."

"I would have worded it differently, but when it comes to dealing with people in general, and especially the opposite sex, I've learned the benefit of being upfront. Even when the cards are placed squarely on the table there is still no guarantee against hard feelings. But at least I know I've been as honest as possible, without anyone being purposely misled."

Ryan nodded. "Thank you."

"You're upset."

"No, really, I'm not. I appreciate your honesty. It's all too rare these days." She turned more fully toward him. "To be clear, you and I are on the exact same page where tonight is concerned. I think you're hot. You said I was, too. We're attracted to each other and want to have fun. I'm not looking for anything else, including more physical encounters beyond tonight. I'm not looking for a relationship, a sugar daddy, a baby daddy or a husband. I've just started a business, and will have very little focus to place elsewhere. If you don't have condoms, we'll need to make a pit stop. After we've...

enjoyed the evening, I'd like a ride home. I'd also like whatever happens to remain between us. Dennis especially doesn't need to know about it. Does that just about cover it?"

"Harshly, but yes."

"You wanted all the cards to be put on the table."

"I would have placed them down gently, maybe added a flashy little spin to the ace or the joker."

"And here I come and slap 'em down like we're playing bid whist and I'm headed to Boston. Then again, you probably don't even know that card game."

"I'm familiar." He smiled, briefly, before turning serious again. "As for your brother or anyone else for that matter, I'm a very private person. I don't kiss and tell."

"Good to know."

Adam eyed her for a long moment. "You're a different kind of woman, Ryan. I like it. It feels good to speak plainly, like we're doing. There's too much time spent in life playing games."

"Depends on what kind of game." Ryan had just begun to lean back into him when they reached the gates of the Breedlove estate. The car stopped, its headlights illuminating the opening of the majestic wrought iron wonders.

"You live here?"

"My entire family lives here."

"Oh." Adam heard trepidation.

"But not in the same house."

"Oh!" He heard relief.

The car drove through the gates and down the wide, winding road. Even in semidarkness the landscape looked grand, lanterns attached to the poles of white picket fences, trees creating dancing shadows as they bent with the wind. Adam watched as Ryan once again displayed a sort of vulnerable wonder that tapped on an unknown place inside his heart. She was quiet as he joked with the driver before they said goodbye and walked up the steps. He opened the door and stood back.

"After you, my lady. Welcome to my home."

Ryan walked inside and stopped just inside the foyer. "You're the only one who lives here?"

Adam nodded. "I have help that comes and goes. But tonight, it's just you and me."

He took her hand, walked them through the house and into the master suite. After hours of flirting and teasing and mental foreplay, it was time to get down to business.

"Your place is beautiful," she said, looking around.

Still holding her hand, Adam walked to the bed and sat down. "I'll give you the tour tomorrow," he whispered as he gently pulled her to his lap. "But I need something else tonight."

The kisses, already hot, wet, deep and searching, quickly gave way to more in-depth pursuits. Adam lay on the bed and pulled Ryan with him, tongues twirling in lips still locked together. He pushed away silky material to caress silkier thighs. His hand moved from there to squeeze the plump cheeks that he adored and back to the triangular patch of lace covering her paradise. When he ran a finger over the material and down her folds, she groaned, tightened her arms and deepened the kiss. Clearly, he was headed in the right direction, a fact further sealed when he slipped a finger beneath the fabric and felt her dewy lips. His sex thickened and lengthened. Any clothes at all was too much of a barrier.

"Hold on, baby." He sat up. "Let me help you out of that."

He gathered the hem of her dress. She raised her

arms. He pulled the material over her head, cupped the weighty globes that greeted him and brushed his fingers across breasts that were barely concealed. He reached for the thin piece of fabric adhered to her skin, gently pulled and revealed a nipple that put the most scrumptious blackberry to shame. He kissed it, pulled off the other cover, and kissed that nipple, too. His shaft was fully engorged now, his control paper-thin. He rolled off the bed, removed his clothes, reached inside the nightstand drawer and put a box of condoms on the table.

Ryan pulled off her undies as she cocked a brow. "Think you have enough?" she asked.

He sheathed himself, then crawled back on the bed and between her legs. "If not, I'll buy more tomorrow."

When it came to making love to Ryan there was so much more that he wanted to do, intended to do, needed to do. He wanted to draw out the foreplay, lick every inch of her skin. But his body had a mind of its own. Ryan spreading her legs beneath him didn't help. He rubbed his sex against her softness before touching his tip to her door. She swiveled her hips beneath him. He sank farther down. Pulling out to the tip, he kissed her, slowly thrusting forward and back. He pulled and plunged, repeating the move until fully engulfed, deeply and completely, until all of him belonged to Ryan. He felt her muscles clench and her body expand as he placed his hands beneath her booty to go deeper still. She clasped her legs around him, brought out goose bumps by lightly running her nails over his flesh. He set up a rhythm—swirling, grinding, pumping—that took them to a magical heaven, over and again.

"That was amazing," Adam said, once his breathing returned to normal. "Even better than I imagined. Was it good for you, too?"

Ryan turned fully toward him, wiped away a bead of sweat. "So much so that I want seconds."

Adam said nothing, just reached for the condoms and prepared for another round. Somewhere from the back of his mind came Ryan's words about no further physical encounters after tonight. Of course she was right. This shouldn't go further. As the sister of a potential employee it couldn't go on. He looked into her eyes while idly flicking her nipple with his finger, and realized just how difficult it would be to not have any more physical contact with Ryan. Maybe impossible, even. But keeping his distance was the right thing to do. So he would try.

Seven

In the days that followed her night with Adam, keeping her feelings toward him casual was easier said than done. One errant thought, and Ryan's body would tingle as it had when he'd touched her. At night, her muscles remembered and clenched like he was still inside her. There was nothing blasé or inconsequential about what they'd shared. From the time he'd picked her up in that fancy limo until he'd dropped her off in an even cooler sports car, every moment had been special. There was nothing casual about that evening, or about Adam Breedlove. It's the reason why even though they hadn't spoken since then, he was still on her mind. Why she had mixed emotions about going to Bakersfield the coming Friday, when she'd see him again.

Having a business to open helped. It kept her busy and focused, thinking about others instead of herself. People who were hurting and needed the type of healing that she could provide. As she pulled into the parking lot of their newly updated establishment, Ryan was determined to keep the reason she'd come back to Las Vegas in the first place front and center in her mind.

Ryan parked in a space near the new office and let out a yelp. Brooklyn had called last night saying the signage was finished, but she didn't know it had been mounted. A smile of satisfaction clung to her face as she exited her car, her eyes never leaving the window. Once in front of the classy artwork of white-and-gold lettering against a backdrop of deep blue, she stopped and took it in:

THE INTEGRATIVE HEALING GROUP
FOR MIND, BODY, SOUL
Brooklyn Chase, CSP, CHT * Ryan Washington, ND

Whole Food Nutrition,
Energy Healing–Prana, Reiki
Massage Therapy, Hypnotherapy, Acupuncture
Intuitive/Angel Reading, EFT Calibration

The sound of a blaring car horn caused Ryan to jump. She turned and waved as Brooklyn pulled up in her canary yellow Kia Sportage complete with airbrushed angel wings. What a woo-woo chick! Ryan loved her like the sister she'd always wanted but never had.

Brooklyn jumped out of the car and ran up to Ryan. "Isn't it beautiful?" she exclaimed, pulling her sister/friend/business partner into an enthusiastic hug. The women danced around like little girls before Ryan pulled out the brand-new, sparkly gold office key.

"Let's take this party inside," she murmured, "before we scare away our clients."

The women stopped just inside the door and took in the foyer/waiting room specifically designed to bring immediate peace and calm to all who entered. The soothing shades of blue, warm lighting and gently flowing fountain created the desired effect. Abstract pictures, a table containing magazines and pamphlets, and three chairs completed the look.

"What do you think?" Ryan asked.

"Hmm…" Brooklyn did a slow turn around the room. "I think we need one more thing."

"What?"

"Some type of aromatherapy."

"An essential oil diffuser!"

"Exactly," Brooklyn said with a nod.

The women high-fived and continued down the short hall with rooms on both sides.

Ryan stopped at the second door on the left and opened it. "I'm glad we decided to rent out these two extra rooms," she said.

Brooklyn followed her into the room. "I agree. I'm still thanking the angels that Suyin replied so quickly."

"I think her acupuncture practice will do really well. But do you think this room will be big enough for her table?"

Brooklyn nodded. "I think so. She'll have that, maybe a chair and a place to set her equipment. What else will she need?"

"I don't know." Ryan pulled out her phone to type notes. "But I'll set up a time for her to come check it out so she'll know exactly what's needed."

They left the small office and continued viewing the rest of the space, taking notes on what decorating items were left to be purchased.

"How's your love life?" Brooklyn asked her as they

reached what they'd planned as a break room, in an abrupt segue from a conversation involving bamboo plants.

"What love life?"

"With Hollywood, that guy who took you to the show at CANN."

"Oh, Adam," Ryan replied, a yawn the only prop missing from her attempt at sounding bored. "That was one date. He isn't my love life."

"I googled him."

"You what?"

"Yep." Brooklyn crossed her arms and calmly leaned against the counter. "Sure did. Put his name in the search engine. Picture came right up. That man is fifty-two kinds of gorgeous, darlin'. His family owns the CANN Casino Hotel and Spa. He's freakin' rich!"

"And?"

"And when are you seeing him again?"

"Friday."

"My girl!" Brooklyn held up her hand.

"But just as friends. We're not going to date."

"Please. Tell that to someone who hasn't seen how good he looks. Talk about balancing your kundalini with a little tantra…"

"Shut up!"

"Why?" Brooklyn asked.

Ryan laughed. Brooklyn didn't. "I'm happy for you, okay?"

"This isn't what you think. Adam's a casual acquaintance, my brother's friend. Neither he nor I are interested in anything serious. We've both got way more important things on our plates."

"There's nothing more important than love, Ryan."

Ryan gave her best friend a patient look, as one might

a child. "That sounds good, but love isn't going to pay the lease on this office."

"And this business, no matter how successful, will never hug you, love you, or keep you warm at night. One needs balance to be truly happy—work, play and love."

Ryan didn't respond. She headed back down the hall toward the foyer.

Brooklyn walked alongside. "Hey, maybe you guys can come to Johnny's concert on Friday. It's a battle of the bands. Should be fun."

"Sounds like it, but we'll be in Bakersfield."

"Meeting the family already! Wow, that is huge!"

"No, this is business! Adam might give my brother a job. He'll be in Bakersfield to tour the plant where Dennis currently works. I'll be there to see Mom and Dad."

Mentioning her adoptive father tempered the mood. "How is he, Ryan?"

"About the same, I guess."

"He's agreed to your treatments, right?" Ryan nodded. Brooklyn reached out and placed a compassionate hand on Ryan's arm. "I'll be sending love and light as well. I hope that they help."

"Me, too."

"And I hope that your brother gets the job. Just remember that contrary to popular belief, business can be mixed with pleasure. A soul mate can show up anytime, anywhere. If it knocks, Ryan, answer it. Take a chance on love."

Adam had offered to book Ryan on a flight to Bakersfield. Tempting, but she'd declined. It didn't feel right to have him spending money on her, even if he was a billionaire. Besides, the drive from Vegas to Bakersfield was just over four hours. She enjoyed short road trips. They helped her relax, gave her time to think and get her head right. For a weekend in the Washington household that included dinner with her lover, a healing session with her father and the first time seeing her mom since a visit with her birth mom, the woman that Ida had forbidden her to see, she'd need it.

That Friday she filled up her tank and left Vegas just after rush hour, arriving at her parents' home around two. She pulled luggage and her laptop out of the car and headed toward the front door. She hadn't always gotten along with the people who'd adopted her, but they were her parents and it had been a while since she'd seen them. Even with the turmoil that surrounded each visit, in the moment, it felt good to be home.

Ryan rang the bell, and then bent down to search for the spare key always hidden beneath the welcome rug. The door opened.

"Oh, hi, Mom."

"Ryan, your hair!" Ida exclaimed, before turning abruptly to walk back down the hall.

Ryan hid an eye roll as she followed her mother, Ida Marie, inside. She'd traded perms for her natural curls her first year of college. But every greeting was as though her mom saw them for the first time.

Ida Marie Washington was a formidable woman, more in comportment than appearance though she was plus-size. Ida wasn't particularly attractive but she worked with what she had. Ryan could count the times on both hands and maybe a foot that she'd seen her mother without makeup or properly dressed in more than twenty years, usually in a color scheme involving black, navy or tan. Outside, she wore low-heeled pumps. Inside, black ballet-type house shoes. No exceptions. Ryan often wondered about the rigidity, what her adoptive mother held on to so tightly. What nurturing or healing needed to happen with Ida's inner child.

"Baby girl!"

Ryan left her luggage at the living room entrance and hurried over to hug her dad. Where Ida was cold and icy, Joe Washington was warmth and comfort. An introspective man with a quiet demeanor and ready smile, he'd often been the salve soothing Ida's barbs and Dennis's taunts. When Ida would get angry and question why she'd bothered to adopt Ryan, Joe would pull her to the side and say, "You are this home's sunshine. Don't let nobody dim that light." She'd loved him every day that she'd known him, and would love him into forever.

"How are you, Dad?" Ryan perched on the arm of the recliner her father occupied, keeping her smile bright despite the shock of noticing her dad's continued weight loss.

"Better now!"

Ida entered the room and sat on the couch. "Don't sit on the arm of the chair like that. Have you forgotten how you were raised?"

Much of it, yes, thankfully. "Sorry, Mom."

Still holding her father's hand, she sat cross-legged on the floor beside him and began inconspicuously doing energy work, as they talked.

"How's Vegas working out for you, Ryan?"

"Things are going well. My business partner and I found a space for our practice and will open in two weeks."

Ryan hung on to her father's "That's great, baby," while trying to ignore Ida's "Practice? Please."

"We've been marketing for clients for well over a month now and already have an almost full first week on the schedule. The final push begins when I get back on Monday. It's a lot of work but…fingers crossed!"

"Had you gone into nursing, a sensible profession, you wouldn't have to beat the pavement for clients. They'd come to you right through the hospital's front door."

"When the Raiders get there in a year or so, you'll have all kinds of injuries to heal," Joe offered.

"Absolutely, Dad! Don't think I haven't already put together a proposal. You know I've always been a Chargers fan but my favorite color is green so…"

The two laughed as Ryan repeated a statement Joe often used in discussing one of their favorite subjects. Dennis preferred basketball. Ida didn't do sports. Joe and Ryan had bonded on long-ago Sundays, watching football and eating popcorn sprinkled with hot sauce, another shared love.

"Give me your other hand, Dad."

"What are you doing?" Ida asked. "And why is your luggage still in the entryway?"

"I forgot all about that," Ryan said, getting up off the floor. And to her dad, "Be right back."

She crossed where her mother sat on the couch, then stopped and turned around. "Maneuvering that bulky luggage inside I didn't even get a hug," she said, bending down to place her arms around her mom's neck. "Are those new earrings? I like them."

"You won't see me in much of anything new anymore," Ida said, after a light pat on Ryan's back. "With Joe on disability, money is tight."

"I'm so sorry for what you and Dad are going through, Mom. It must be a very difficult adjustment."

"Hmph."

Ryan grabbed the handle of her luggage and headed

toward the stairs. She reached the second floor of the place she'd called home from the time she was nine until two weeks after turning eighteen. She tried the knob on her old bedroom door and was surprised to find it locked. Moving on to the smaller room, she opened the door. A daybed had replaced the double that Dennis used when he'd returned there after leaving the military. The bedding was cream-colored, giving the room a lighter feel. Dennis preferred black, so the change was stark. Ryan liked it. She pulled her luggage into the room, placed her computer bag on the bed and then in a reversion back to the curious child she'd always been, she grabbed a bobby pin from the hallway bathroom and opened the other room's locked door.

One step inside and Ryan stopped short. The place was a mess. Boxes were everywhere, along with clothes she assumed belonged to Dennis strewn all over the place. Had he moved back home? She walked into the room, trying to figure out the mystery as she looked around. She lifted the lids of a couple boxes. One contained files and other loose paper. With just the slightest twinge of little-sister guilt, she knelt and began flipping through files, all from Bakersfield Meat Packing. Further, intrigued, Ryan looked through the folders more closely and pulled out one labeled H&R. On top of the pile was a formal-looking letter dated three weeks ago.

Dear Mr. Washington:

This letter shall serve as official notice that you have been terminated from...effective immediately...

Ryan sat back on her haunches. WTH? How was Dennis giving Adam a tour of a plant where he no longer worked? Hearing feet on the staircase, she hurriedly returned the folder to the box, slapped on the lid and exited the room, careful to lock the door behind her, just as Ida reached the top of the stairs.

"What are you doing?" she asked.

Ryan had a question, too. "Has Dennis moved back home? That bedroom door is locked."

Ida walked to the door and tried unsuccessfully to open it. "As it happens, your brother will soon be joining you in Las Vegas. He's been recruited for a high-level management job with CANN International, a billion-dollar company."

Is that what he told you?

"You need to get yourself a real job, Ryan. When this project you're working on fails to make money, your dad and I won't be able to help you."

Ida continued on to the master bedroom at the end of the hall. It was just as well. Far be it from Ryan to correct whatever information Dennis had told her. Of more interest to Ryan was what Dennis had told Adam, and why he'd been terminated from his job. Ryan tried to tell herself it was none of her business. Then she remembered tonight and Adam coming for dinner, and knew that as much as she wanted to wash her hands of what felt like sneaky shenanigans, Dennis had her all up in the mix.

Eight

Adam felt it as soon as the door opened, an air of tension and discomfort despite the bright smile from the woman who opened the door.

"Hello, son." The woman gave Dennis an enthusiastic hug while eyeing Adam appreciatively. She released him and held out her hand. "Hello, I'm Ida Washington, Dennis's mom. You must be Adam."

"Yes, ma'am." Adam offered a firm grip and a smile as he shook her hand. "It's very nice to meet you."

"Come on in, you two."

Dennis lifted his nose. "Something smells good."

They entered the living room. "It sure does. Mrs. Washington, I told Dennis that your cooking dinner was totally unnecessary, but I appreciate it."

"It was no bother and, please, call me Ida."

"Thank you."

Adam took in the stately woman who escorted them

into the room. Ryan didn't look like her mother at all. He looked for her features in the neatly dressed man sitting in a recliner. Both had smooth cocoa skin and high cheekbones. But the big doe-like eyes, pert nose, full lips and sweet curves seemed to be uniquely Ryan's, one of a kind.

"Hey, Dad." Dennis gave his dad a pat on the shoulder. "You remember Adam, a friend from high school? His family owns CANN International."

Adam shook the older man's hand. "Nice to see you again, Joe."

"He owns a cattle ranch, too. That's why he's in Bakersfield, to take a look at the plant that I run. He's looking for a manager for the one he's building. Looks like I might be joining Ryan back in Vegas."

Dennis looked around. "Is she here? I saw her car."

"She'll be down momentarily," Ida said. "Have a seat, you two. Dinner is almost ready."

As Adam walked over to sit on the couch, he felt her before he saw her. A subtle change in the atmosphere, like a ray of sun breaking through clouds, before Ryan walked into the room. He looked up as she entered wearing a colorful oversize sweater with bright red leggings, her bouncy curls wild and free, and felt comfortable for the first time since entering the home.

"Ryan." He quickly stood, an instinctive move, and given the reactions it elicited, one he instantly regretted. Dennis's eyes traveling between them as his expression grew smug. Ida stopping midstride, a slight frown on her face before she realized it and took her look neutral. The only one who had a reaction he understood was Joe. He beamed, as though Ryan was the beat of his heart.

He pushed his hands into his pockets, tried to look nonchalant. "Hey."

"Hey, Adam!" Her hug was brief, but he felt a shakiness to the hand that squeezed his arm after. She turned to Dennis, clapped him on the shoulder. "What's up, brother?"

"You, I guess, the way Adam jumped up to greet you."

"No, man, that's just how I was raised, to get up when a woman enters the room."

"They're called manners," Ryan teased. "Those practiced by gentlemen, which is probably why you didn't recognize them."

"Whatever," Dennis replied, without further comeback to the rare and nicely placed barb.

He looked unconvinced, but Ida, who hadn't moved from where she'd stopped on her way to the kitchen, finally continued around the corner.

"I'm going to help Mom set the table," Ryan said.

She left and Adam would swear that just a bit of his air left the room. He'd hoped that the intense feelings he'd experienced since their night together would have abated. It was one reason why he hadn't called her until yesterday, and then only to offer the plane ticket. He'd been with women more beautiful, more successful, and with Ryan being a vegetarian while he butchered what most Americans ate for dinner, more evenly matched as well. After how his body had reacted just now Ryan clearly had him under a spell. Unfortunately it would have to be broken. She was too beautiful to be hidden, too special to be treated as a casual friend. But dalliances were all he had time for right now. He was focused on helping to run a family empire while building another successful business that was all his own.

It wasn't long before the men were called to dinner.

As they sat and Ida and Ryan brought in the rest of the dishes, the doorbell rang.

"Who's that?" Ryan asked, taking the seat across from Adam.

Ida entered with the last covered dish and placed it on the remaining trivet. "Probably Luke." She took a seat at the head of the table. "He has a sixth sense when it comes to my cooking and showing up just in time to eat."

Dennis returned to the table with Luke, whom Adam had met while at the plant. Dennis had introduced him as a friend and colleague he'd known practically all of his life. Luke was a nice-looking guy who cleaned up well. The dirty jeans and stained T-shirt from earlier had been replaced with a casual tan-colored suit and a black V-neck pullover. Adam could tell that the clothing he wore was of a high quality and didn't miss the diamond stud that winked from his ear.

"Miss Ida! Papa Joe!" Luke walked over and shook hands with Joe, then moved on to give Ida a hug. Joe's greeting to Luke was enthusiastic but Adam noted Ida's was fairly cool, but then again given her personality, maybe not.

He looked at Ryan, stopped and took a step back. "Ryan, wow," he said, slowly shaking his head as he ogled her in a way that to Adam skirted precariously close to disrespect, although Adam knew his observation might be biased. He had no claim to Ryan but in the moment could imagine how Tarzan felt if someone hit on Jane.

"It's been a long time."

"Yes, it has."

Über observant by nature, Adam didn't miss how before Luke got anywhere close, Ryan held out a stiff arm for a handshake instead of a hug. Her lips smiled. Her eyes didn't. She looked most uncomfortable. Adam made a note to find out why.

"I didn't think you could get any prettier," Luke said, "but I was wrong. Don't you have a birthday coming up soon?"

"In a week," Dennis responded, with a frown that was only partially mocking. "And no, you can't buy her a present, or be her present."

Luke laughed. To Adam, it sounded forced. He didn't think Luke found the comment funny. It was the first time he'd heard Dennis actually defend his sister. He had no way of knowing it, but that boded well for Dennis potentially being hired to work at Breedlove Beef.

Luke took the seat beside Adam. Dinner service began. Ida lifted the lid from the main dish, smothered chicken and gravy. "It's not the fancy food you're used to, Adam," she said, spinning the utensils on the rotating serving dish toward him. "But I hope you enjoy it."

"Oh, I like good food, Mrs. Washington, Ida, fancy or not." He placed a hearty serving on his plate. "And this smells super good."

"Mom can burn," Dennis said, taking the ladle Adam offered.

"She is an excellent cook," Ryan said.

"How do you know?" Ida asked. "You don't eat my cooking."

"I don't eat the dishes you fix that contain meat," Ryan replied. "But my mouth watered as I brought those candied yams to the table, and your mac and cheese will probably keep me eating dairy for life!"

"You always did like that dish," Ida said with a smile that suggested Ryan's compliment pleased her. "Dennis will eat anything I put in front of him, including the plate I imagine, if he were hungry enough. I can say there's less fried foods and fat in our diet. We are trying to eat healthier now."

Luke and Dennis led the bulk of conversation as other lids were lifted and plates filled. Adam noticed that other than the chicken, which was some of the best he'd ever put in his mouth, the other dishes seemed to be ones that Ryan could eat.

"Is this your first time in Bakersfield?" Joe asked as he reached for a glass of sweet tea.

"On the way up that's something I was trying to remember," Adam said. "As a young kid I traveled all over California with my dad, so it's highly likely that I was here, but a long time ago."

"Bakersfield isn't the most memorable city in the Golden State," Joe continued. "But it's an agricultural hub. So you're raising cattle now?"

"I thought your family owned a hotel." Ida looked from Adam to Dennis, clearly confused.

"They do, Mom," Dennis said. "In fact, they own several, all over the world. But Adam has other interests, ones that will complement the hotel business. He's an entrepreneur. Right, Adam?"

"A component of Breedlove Ranch is complementary to the hotel enterprise. The cattle I raise will be used in many of our restaurants."

"Oh," Ida said. "That's nice."

"More than nice, Mom," Dennis said. "He's raising the highest-quality beef one can get in this country. Have you heard of Kobe beef?"

"Of course."

"His will be high quality like that."

"And Dennis will be working with you?" Ida asked.

"I hope so," Dennis interjected. "Both me and Luke."

Adam set down his fork and wiped his mouth with a napkin. "We're in the final phases of constructing a plant on the ranch and are looking for the right person to manage it. Running into Dennis and finding out that's his niche definitely put him in the running, and after touring the plant he manages here, I'm even more impressed. But the decision isn't solely up to me. The choice will be made by the team."

"You own the company," Dennis said. "The buck is supposed to stop with you!"

"The buck does," Adam replied, smiling. "But not this decision. Whoever takes this job will have a ton of responsibility on their shoulders, and will work closely with the ranch manager and department supervisors. Running a ranch is complex, definitely a group effort. Experience, education, skill, that all counts. But so does making sure the fit of one is right for the whole."

Dennis made a show of puffing his chest and bulging his arms like Superman. "I can handle it."

Everyone laughed except Ryan, but Adam did see the glimpse of a smile.

"I told him that Ryan was looking for a job. She wasn't interested, though, being that she doesn't eat meat and all."

"Is that true?" Ida asked. Her voice was pleasant, but Adam noticed a slight change in her demeanor, a difference between her interactions with her daughter compared to how she treated her son. "I would think that working for someone affiliated with a corporation as large as the CANN hotels would be a huge opportunity."

"I'm more impressed with what Ryan is doing," Adam said, "using her education and training to help people heal. I never paid much attention to the connection between what we eat and how we feel, but it makes total sense."

Luke cleaned a chicken bone and unashamedly licked his fingers. "Then I must be 100 percent healthy because this chicken is making me feel good!"

"You seem to know quite a bit about Ryan," Joe said to Adam. "The two of you know each other from high school, too?"

"No, sir. I didn't even know Dennis had a sister."

"She tagged along the day I met Adam for lunch," Dennis said. "Some things never change," he said, shaking his head. "The next day he called and asked for her home number, so…"

"It was business," Ryan quickly interjected. "Adam wants to offer healthy alternatives on his menu, a conversation that came up at the lunch Dennis mentioned. Remember, Denny?"

"Yep, I remember."

"That's why he wanted to contact me."

Adam felt something soft, tickly, slowly moving up his leg. He was seconds away from slapping away what he could only think was an insect when the "bug" tapped him, and he realized it was Ryan's big toe.

"We've talked, a couple times at length, about ways we can prepare food that is nourishing and still completely delicious," she said.

The little minx! Had she any idea how long it had taken for him to get a handle on his hormones after she'd walked into the room? And here now, with every word from that sweet little mouth, the testosterone was buzzing again. Still, he enjoyed the subtle flirting. It reminded him of the wonderful time they'd had Tuesday night. The trip to Bakersfield had been interesting, to say the least. There would be a lot to process when he went home. But when it came to Ryan there was nothing to think about. His feelings were clear. He needed to see her again, to wrap his arms around her softness, feel her breath in his ear and hear her breathy whimpers as he gave her pleasure. One more time. One more night into the morning. After that she'd be Dennis's sister, a platonic friend, maybe a consultant to his restaurant… nothing more.

Nine

Ryan got the first text on Friday night, less than an hour after the guys had left her parents' home—Adam headed to the airport, Dennis and Luke no doubt went to the nearest bar for the most accommodating women. For Ryan, Luke couldn't leave her sight soon enough, but she missed Adam already. She'd volunteered to do dinner cleanup to keep herself busy and her mind distracted, and was loading the dishwasher when her phone vibrated.

You looked beautiful tonight.

She'd hurriedly replied. You looked good, too.

You looked good, smelled good, felt good. Running your toe up my leg like that? You were being a very bad girl.

The message made her giggle. The look in Adam's eyes after she'd done it made her think he might be feeling what she was feeling, but with the other company present she couldn't be sure. Until now. The attraction continued to be mutual. She sent a smiley face.

When are you back in Vegas?

Monday.

Why not Sunday? I want to see you.

It wasn't what they'd planned. But getting together again is what they both wanted. Even so, her reply was noncommittal. Maybe.

When Ryan saw Dennis in his room the next morning, Adam's text and their plans for the following day were still on her mind. So was his suggestion that Luke be hired, too. She could understand Dennis wanting to help out a friend but nothing she knew about Luke made her think that hiring him would be a good idea. She'd stayed quiet at dinner but today was different. She and Dennis needed to talk.

"What a mess," she said, her mood deceptively light as she entered his room. "I thought military guys were neat freaks."

"I thought you knew about manners but I didn't hear you knock."

"That's because the door was open." She plopped down on the unmade bed. "When did you move back home?"

"A little while ago."

The tone of his answer conveyed his annoyance, but Ryan plowed on undeterred. "Why?" No answer.

She needed to push, so she slid off the bed and walked over to where the boxes she'd rummaged through were stacked against the wall. "Is it because you're no longer working at the plant?"

Dennis turned around with a scowl on his face. "Who says I'm not working there?"

"Mom did. She thought you were already hired in Vegas." Ryan closed the bedroom door and leaned against it. "But I saw the paperwork in one of those boxes. You didn't quit, either. You got fired."

Though her statement was explosive, her voice remained low and calm. Dennis's did not.

"What the hell were you doing snooping in my things?"

"It wasn't intentional. I came back to my old room and found all of this crap in it. Opened a couple boxes to see what was in there."

Dennis shrugged. "Big deal."

"Does Adam know you were fired?"

"Get out of my room!"

"Shh! You'll wake Mom and Dad." Ryan felt her brother's anger but still needed answers. "I just wondered how you gave him a tour of a place where you no longer worked."

"What's it to you? Mind your own business!"

"This became my business the day you invited me to lunch!" Ryan stopped and took a breath. Getting angry, or loud, would not be productive. "Look, I don't want to fight with you. I just don't want to be a part of whatever you're scheming."

"I'm not scheming."

"You're trying to get Luke a job with Adam. I don't like him."

"Who asked you?"

"Nobody. But if Adam asks for my opinion, I'll tell him the truth."

"You'll keep your mouth shut," Dennis snarled, his volume rising with every word. "Now…get out of my room!"

The door opened as Ryan turned to leave. It was Ida. Her eyes zeroed in on Ryan. She didn't look happy.

"What is all of this yelling about?" she demanded, glaring at Ryan even though Dennis had yelled. "Why are you bothering him?"

"She's trying to sabotage my opportunity with Adam," Dennis answered. "I think she wants him all to herself."

Ryan couldn't help but laugh. "That's ridiculous."

"It sure is," Ida said. "I saw you trying to impress him last night. But that boy's way above your pay grade."

"She's upset that I'm moving to Vegas and that Luke might come with me. If Adam asks her about Luke she said her answer won't be good."

"I said if asked I would give my opinion."

"He knows Luke and I are tight. If you bad-mouth him, what would that say about me?"

"What would it say about me if I lied about how I feel about Luke?"

"You've never cared for that boy," Ida said, her eyes narrowing as she glared at Ryan. "I never understood why."

"That's because you can't know what it's like to be teased about being adopted."

"I told you then to pay him no mind, yet what he said all those years ago is still on yours? So, you were adopted. So what? We gave you a family and this is how you thank us? By being upset that someone pointed it out a time or two, a kid who was known for teasing? Yet here you are playing the victim. Do you think you're the only one who suffered?"

Ryan clamped her mouth shut. If she opened it to answer, she might not be able to control what else flowed out.

"I tell you what. You weren't. I suffered plenty more than you. And I'll tell you another thing. You'd better not mess things up for Dennis. Because when it comes to opinions, there are some that can be shared that would mess up your life, too."

Soon after, Dennis stormed out of the house. Her mother wasn't far behind him. Since her father's diagnosis Ida had taken on more hours, often working at the Postal Service's processing plant on Saturday afternoons. Neither spoke another word to her before they left, though she heard mumbling that included her name. With a skill honed over a lifetime of verbal abuse, Ryan locked away what happened to be processed later and went in search of her father. She wanted to do a session of energy healing while the house was quiet and knew that helping to ease or take away some of his discomfort would lessen her emotional pain.

Ryan's dad rarely got involved in their mother-daughter arguments, but he was often her refuge once they were done. He had a way of comforting the adopted daughter without bashing his wife. Today was no exception.

"Ida is like a mama bear when it comes to Dennis," he began, after lying facedown on the portable table that Ryan had covered with a thick memory foam pad. "It's always been that way. She lashes out, but she doesn't mean it."

"The words hurt just the same."

Ryan began the treatment. The fluid Reiki movements over her adoptive dad's body brought calm to her spirit. She allowed the prior conversation to float back into her mind. She listened to the mental replay dispassionately, hearing the pain beneath Ida's caustic words.

"I wonder why Mom adopted me," she softly mused.

"Because she loves you," Joe answered.

"Maybe so, but she doesn't like me very much."

"Sometimes she doesn't like me, either, and I've been married to the woman for more than thirty years." He winked and lay back down on the table. It was Ryan's first smile all day.

Ryan finished the intensive healing session with Joe. Afterward, they enjoyed a leisurely brunch. Ryan was by no means a cook, but her veggie-filled omelet was cheesy and spicy, and one-on-one time with her father was better than any meal. She didn't spend the night though as originally planned, but headed back to Las Vegas before Ida returned home. Ryan felt conflicted on so many levels. She needed time to process everything from the past twenty-four hours—her Adam attraction, the Dennis dilemma, her loathing for Luke and the Ida enigma. Those problems were ones she'd have to figure out on her own. But there was someone who could help with a piece missing from her life—her birth father. She left Bakersfield for Las Vegas and a visit with her birth mom, Phyllis Moore.

The visit didn't go as planned. They'd met in person only a handful of times, awkward prison visits. Scant emails and short phone calls were hardly building blocks for a mother-daughter relationship. Ryan realized she'd expected too much.

"Can you tell me anything about my father?"

"Not really."

"You don't have anything, not even a name?"

"I've got several names, none that you need. Why learn something about a man you've never met?"

"Because he's my dad."

"He's the man who knocked me up and kept on walking. Let the past stay there!"

"I have a right to know where I come from," Ryan replied, near tears.

Phyllis seemed moved, but the brief moment passed.

"Who it was doesn't matter. Nothing you find out now can change what happened back then."

"It will change me," Ryan had countered. "Learning of your addiction helped me understand why I was abandoned. Hearing about your back problem and the prolonged use of prescription medication that led to the opioid addiction provided a reason I was put in foster care, one that replaced the one believed until then—that I wasn't a person worth loving."

"You knew how I felt. Loving you is why I let the Washingtons adopt you. I knew they could give you what I couldn't."

Ryan had asked her mother about the relationship with Ida, whether she'd known her beforehand and why they didn't get along.

"She discouraged me from looking for you," Ryan explained. "Why would she do that?"

"Because you already had a mother," Phyllis replied. "One is all you need. Leave the past alone, Ryan, and live in the moment."

The visit ended with Ryan feeling almost as though she'd been abandoned again. Yet after a good night's sleep and some leisurely shopping, she'd decided to take Phyllis's advice and live in the moment by having one more romp with Adam before breaking off all romantic contact. Out of the market and back in her car, she engaged her Bluetooth, then merged into the light Sunday-morning traffic.

"Where are you?" was his greeting.

"Hello to you, too." His voice warmed her heart.

Adam laughed. "Hello, gorgeous. Where are you?"

"Near Red Rock."

"Cool, you're not far from the hotel. Can you meet me there?"

"Why?"

"I've got something for you."

"Really? What?"

"It's a surprise."

The sexiness in his voice was as thick as molasses that she could imagine oozing wet and sticky down her bare skin, much as Adam's tongue had the one time they'd been together. The slow way he spoke, raspy and low, should have been illegal. At the very least he should have been required to register a voice like that as a lethal weapon. But if that happened, Ryan thought, she needed to be arrested, too. Because becoming that aroused by nothing more than consonants and vowels should be against the law.

"I just spent an hour at the farmer's market. Maybe I should go home and shower first."

"I know you've never stayed there but we have showers in every suite. I'll text you the room number and leave a special card key for you at the front desk. See you soon?"

"Yes."

"I can't wait."

Ryan reached the CANN Casino Hotel and Spa

and as Adam had instructed in the text he'd sent, she stopped at the valet booth. From there until she arrived at the elevator, the service she received was stellar, the best she'd ever experienced at a hotel or anywhere. Was this what it felt like to be wealthy? Knowing this was the first and last time she'd experience such luxury was bittersweet.

Adam had directed her to a penthouse suite. She got on the elevator and closed her eyes, tried to ignore the pang of fear in her stomach as the car sped upward. Her discomfort with elevators was only part of the reason for her anxiety. She'd bet the money from her first fifty clients that Adam would have questions about his visit to Bakersfield in general and Dennis in particular. He was considering her brother for a very important position and was obviously an excellent businessman. Why wouldn't he ask what she thought about it? And how could she answer without lying, yet not quite tell the truth?

The elevator opened to a small landing with doors on each wall. She went to penthouse A and slid in the card.

"Hello?"

Ryan paused and stepped inside. A beautiful foyer led into a short hall. Soothing music wafted toward her, along with wonderful scents she recognized including jasmine and vanilla. Adam came around the corner, arms outstretched. He was barefoot, and wore gray drawstring pants and a black tank top. Perfect.

"There you are." He pulled Ryan into his body, squeezed her as though she was something exquisite and rare. There was no need for words because their bodies were talking. Ryan's arms slid around his neck as their lips came together. He palmed her butt, pressed her against his already hardening shaft. For several minutes they got no farther than that hallway. By the time he gently took her hand and pulled her into the main living space, her dress had already been removed and left behind on the floor. The room took her breath away.

"This is incredible! Adam, oh my God!"

Ryan had never been overly modest, and something about standing in front of floor-to-ceiling windows in nothing but a thong made her feel powerful, sexy and a little bit naughty. Being over a hundred stories in the air helped, too, she imagined. Adam came up behind her, teasing her nipples into pert attention. His other hand snaked down to her heat between her legs.

"Can anyone see us?" Ryan asked. Posing naked was one thing. Being the unwitting subject of a potential sex tape was something else altogether.

"No, babe. These are one-way windows. We can see out but no one can see in."

She turned in his arms. "Let's take a shower."

They did, and soap and water wasn't the only thing felt on skin. Fingers skimmed. Tongues glided. Ryan's eyes turned mischievous as her knees met the polished stone floor. She encircled Adam's dick with her fingers, flicked her tongue on and around its mushroomed tip. His fingers stroked her hair. She slid wet lips up and down his generous package, slowly at first, then faster, harder, until a strained hiss escaped his mouth and he pulled away. Before Ryan could rise on her own Adam lifted her up, perched her on the bench and placed her legs over his shoulders. She didn't have to wonder what came next because mere seconds passed before her back was against the shower walls and his face was buried in the juncture of her thighs. Had his oral feats been filmed, the video would have definitely gone viral. His tongue was masterful, his fingers relentless, creating an orgasm that shook Ryan from head to toe. He gently lowered her to the bench, stepped out of the shower and returned with a familiar square foil. After making delicious love under the rain forest showerhead, they washed each other's satisfied bodies and tumbled into bed.

"Even better than last time," Ryan murmured, stretching like a satisfied feline. "I think between that tongue—" she kissed his lips "—and those fingers—" she wrapped hers in his "—every muscle in my body was rubbed."

"What can I say? You bring out the beast in me."

There was a knock at the door. Ryan started. "Who's that?"

"Room service." Adam slid off the bed, stepped into a walk-in closet and, once robed, strolled to the front door. Seconds later, he returned wheeling a tray loaded with covered dishes.

"Brunch in bed," he told her. "And guess what? It's all vegetarian."

After retrieving her dress, Ryan rejoined Adam on the bed. If asked she wouldn't have said she was hungry, but one bite of the veggie-filled omelet topped with cashew cheese and she was all in. Adam enjoyed a pecan pie pancake topped with caramelized bananas, dripping with spiced maple syrup.

Ryan took a few bites, then reached for the pitcher of orange juice and poured two glasses. "When it comes to your restaurant and vegetarian options, I don't think you need my help. Just get with the chef who fixed all this."

"Emilio is talented but you're way cuter," Adam teased. He reached for the glass of juice Ryan had poured for him. "Thanks."

"You're welcome."

Adam took a long swig of the juice, then picked up his fork and resumed eating. "I enjoyed meeting your family on Friday," he said after a few bites.

"Even with Dennis trying to stir things up by suggesting there's something between us?"

"It's natural that he'd be curious to see whether or not his plan worked."

"So you picked that up, huh? That he was trying to set us up."

"Bringing a vegetarian to a burger joint made that move fairly obvious. Maybe he'd planned to ask for a job all along and thought bringing along his very pretty sister might improve his chances of getting hired."

"Since we're keeping our rendezvous a secret, he'll never know." Ryan reached for one of the intricately folded linen napkins. "It's funny that you were onto him from the start. I love my brother but sometimes he can be a cad."

"I noticed that. I also got the feeling that he's your mom's favorite while you seem closer to your dad. Am I right?"

"Yes."

"You look more like him, too, although some of your features don't resemble either of them. But I get that. My older brother, Christian, is clearly a Breedlove but looks more like our grandfather than our dad."

Ryan nodded but became very interested in eating. The longer her mouth stayed full the less she'd have to talk.

For a while they ate in silence. "I'm surprised at how delicious this food tastes," he said after finishing off his omelet. "I liked your mom's cooking," he added.

"I used to," Ryan admitted. "Nothing like comfort food." Then because she couldn't stand the feeling of waiting for a hammer to drop, she asked him, "How was your visit to where Dennis works?"

"Interesting," Adam said. He shifted and sat up against the headboard. "The guy who came to dinner, Luke, works there, too. He said the two were as close as brothers and that if there were more openings at the plant, I should give him serious consideration."

Again, Ryan kept silent. The best thing she could say about Luke Johnson was nothing at all.

"What do you think?"

Adam had done the very thing she'd been afraid of—sought out her opinion. "I'm probably not the best person to ask," she finally said.

"You don't like him." His accuracy surprised her. It showed on her face. "I saw your reaction to him the other night."

"No, but it's for personal reasons."

Adam's countenance darkened quickly. "Did he do something to hurt you?"

"No."

"Something unethical?"

Ryan shook her head. "It all happened a long time ago, before I left for college. I hadn't seen him for years."

"I get the feeling you were fine with that, not seeing him."

"I never knew him very well and what I did know… yeah, not impressed."

"The way he eyed you as though you were a barbecued rib made me want to punch him."

Ryan smiled. She knew the statement was made because guys were naturally territorial, not because of any special feelings that he had for her. But it sounded good anyway.

"Dennis knows his way around a slaughterhouse, that's for sure. Their facility is larger than the one we've designed, and handles more livestock. So when it comes to general overall experience, I believe he'd be a good fit."

Ryan nodded.

"What do you think about my hiring him? Is he someone you'd recommend?"

Ryan couldn't tell him what she really thought. So she made light of the moment. "Seriously, you're asking me about someone's qualifications to work in meat-packing?"

"Well, stated that way it does sound crazy." Adam finished his juice, put down the glass and looked beyond her, and it seemed beyond anything he could see from the tall, paneless windows.

"I've always liked your brother, you know?"

"Because he defended you, right?"

"He did."

"Why were the guys teasing you?"

The question was simple but from the subtle yet unmistakable change in Adam's demeanor, the answer was not.

He pinned her with a hard look and said, "Growing up, I suffered from dyslexia. I was almost seventeen years old when it was finally diagnosed."

Ryan saw that it wasn't the man but a little boy that answered, the one that her brother had protected. The pain in his voice hurt her heart. "You have dyslexia," she gently corrected. "But you don't have to suffer from it."

"Why? Do you think you can heal me? Will it go away if I eat the right foods?"

"I don't know," Ryan said. "But I can try to help you."

Adam placed the containers they'd set on the bed back on the tray and pulled the tie on his robe. "I know a way you can help me," he said, once again reaching for the hem of her dress. "And this requires no reading at all."

Ryan had planned to have another conversation, the one where she said this was it and they couldn't see each other romantically anymore. But she followed his lead and allowed the distraction. She understood the need he felt to run away from what shamed him. She'd been forced to do the same. If he discovered her secrets, who knew? Maybe he'd want to get away again…from her.

Ten

Adam stanched a yawn as he entered the barn that contained the offices of Breedlove Ranch. Ryan hadn't left his private hotel suite until Monday dawned. Halfway through forty winks he had to get up to attend a 7:00 a.m. business breakfast, fortunately located in the hotel, followed by one meeting after the next. His late lunch had been a sandwich at his desk while on a conference call with the architects and construction company handling the CANN Island build in Djibouti, an ambitious project dreamed up by his brother Christian and on track to be completed within the next twelve months. He'd handled a slew of correspondence with his secretary before dashing out to not be late for his own meeting. Hiring a manager for the processing plant was top of the agenda. He'd spoken with Stan, the ranch manager, on Friday and sent over Dennis's résumé to be reviewed. He knew there were at least two other

well-qualified candidates in the running. The sooner
the decision was made on who to hire, the better he'd
feel about meeting their projection of shipping out the
first orders of Breedlove Wagyu at the first of the year.

While clearly qualified and Adam's first pick, Dennis wasn't quite the man that Adam remembered. Life
seemed to have hardened the guy he used to call Washboard. A cloud of cynicism hung over his life. Adam
would have liked the opportunity to speak with people
Dennis worked with other than Luke. He didn't doubt
that his old friend was good at his job, but Breedlove
Beef would be no ordinary slaughterhouse. The same
care and attention given to raising the cattle would be
demanded in how the facility was run and how the
meat was processed. A bad batch of beef could ruin a
farm. Quality was everything. Loyalty to the Breedlove brand, paramount. The Dennis from back in the
day had stood up for him and had his back. Would he
have the same devotion to Adam's company and Breedlove Beef? Could he be trusted with the most important
position Adam had to fill since starting the company
five years ago?

Adam took the steps two at a time and entered the
room at the top of the landing. Stan was already there,
along with a few of the company's board members including Wally Martin, Henry Tolliver and his grandmother Jewel's husband, Adam's Native American
stepgrandfather who knew land, cows and horses better than almost anyone, Will Yazzie Breedlove.

Stan, who ran the ranch the way he used to run his
military platoon, made a show of checking his watch.

"You're late."

"I'm a minute early."

"That's what happens when you keep time with a

foreigner's watch. You need one of these." Stan held up his arm to show off a chunky black watch with a thick band. "Something made in America."

"Sure thing," Adam replied, not giving his manager the chance to sing the praises of his country the way he knew Stan wanted to do. The guy was a patriot to his soul, one whom Adam highly respected. It was men like him who filled the forces that helped keep the country safe.

Adam sat down, crossed a leg over his knee and looked around the table. "Okay, let's get right to it. We all know why we're here. We need to hire a plant manager ASAP. On Friday, I visited Bakersfield Meat Packing, managed by an old friend of mine. It's a big operation, larger than ours. I think he'd work well for us. Stan, what were you able to find out on Dennis Washington?"

Stan picked up the paper in front of him. "Looks good on paper, for sure. I appreciate that he's a military man. Nothing too serious came up on his background check. He likes speed and has a number of traffic violations to prove it. His credit isn't the best, which tells us he manages a plant better than he does his bank account. Speaking of the plant, did you know that he no longer works there?"

"No, I didn't. When did he leave, and why?"

"I'm not sure," Stan answered. "HR could confirm that he'd worked there as the manager but for legal reasons wouldn't tell me how or why he left. Luke Johnson, a coworker at the plant and one of his references, says he recently resigned but another source said he was fired."

This information blindsided Adam. Just the Friday before, Dennis had given the tour of Bakersfield Meat as though he owned the place. Had something happened

over the weekend? Did Dennis believe the job at Breedlove was a fait accompli?

"What's your overall impression?" he asked Stan.

"I'm leaning toward the guy from North Dakota.
He's older, more seasoned, a solid cattle rancher. But
there's no denying that when it comes to meatpacking
plants, Dennis Washington knows his stuff."

Discussion continued. Adam listened to everyone's
opinion and then made his decision. They hired Dennis Washington. He told himself that it was because he
knew Dennis, because his old friend was highly qualified and the position must be filled quickly. That he
had a very attractive sister who was never far from his
thoughts had nothing to do with it. That's what he told
himself. But it did.

By the eve of her birthday, Ryan was exhausted.
She'd spent the week traversing one end of Las Vegas to
the other, handing out flyers and setting up her portable
massage chair in malls, stores and casinos to perform
various types of hands-on healing to drum up business
for Integrative Healing. Earlier today she and Brooklyn
had attended an Oktoberfest event. Much of the crowd
had drinking and celebrating on their mind, but Brooklyn's angel readings were popular and Ryan had rubbed
more necks and shoulders than she cared to count. She
turned down an invite from Brooklyn to Johnny's concert, and when Adam texted not long after, said no to
him, too. But now, two hours later, full, showered and
relaxed, she wished she hadn't turned him down so
quickly. Having had a tiring day was only part of it.
The other part of it was feeling the walls closing in on
her. Dennis got the job and was moving to Vegas. Her
mother had left a message to not muck it up for him. If

her adopted mom only knew. Her "mucking" probably helped him get the job! Would his being so close impact her personal decisions of trying to build a relationship with Phyllis and find her birth father?

Ryan decided not to call Adam. Instead, after tossing the phone on the couch, she punched a pillow to put behind her head and grabbed the remote with the hopes of getting lost in someone else's story. The next thing she knew she woke up to find the movie over and the TV watching her. Guess she hadn't needed company after all. She shed her clothes, crawled between the covers and was quickly back asleep.

Hours later, when the doorbell rang, Ryan didn't move immediately. She thought she was dreaming. It rang again. Her eyes blinked open. She looked toward the window, where dim shards of light eased from the space around the edges of the blinds. It was almost still dark outside.

What time is it?

"Just a minute!" Throwing back the covers, Ryan snatched a robe from the foot of the bed and hurried toward the door. One look out the peephole and her heart melted. Someone had sent her flowers!

She opened the door, wondering who could they be from. No one from her family, she knew for sure. Dennis rarely remembered her birthday and she'd received a card from her parents earlier in the week. Brooklyn, maybe?

"Hi."

"Ryan Washington?"

"Yeah, that's me."

"These are for you."

"Wow!" The bouquet was even bigger and more

beautiful than it appeared through the peephole. The vase alone was huge.

"Do you need help getting it inside?"

"No, I think I've got it. Hold on, though, and I'll get you a tip."

"That's already taken care of. Enjoy your day."

Ryan set the arrangement down on the first available table and looked for an envelope. It was hidden within the abundance of greenery. She opened it up and pulled out the card inside it.

Flowers pale in comparison to your beauty, but I hope these will brighten your morning. If you have a couple of hours today, I'd love to spoil you with a little R&R. Call me. Adam.

Ryan took another look at the flowers, bent over and inhaled their heavenly scent. It would be really easy to fall for Adam, she decided. But she couldn't, especially now that Dennis was moving here and they'd be working together so closely. For the best, she decided, returning to her room and flopping on the bed. Getting Integrative Healing off the ground would and should be her singular focus. When trying to build one's own empire, who had time for cowboys?

She fluffed up the pillows behind her, lay back and tapped her cell phone screen. Said cowboy answered at once.

"Good morning, birthday girl!"

"Good morning."

"Or maybe *girl* isn't the right choice. Maybe I should have said birthday woman, or lady."

"I prefer birthday goddess."

"Ha! You are that," Adam replied, his voice slipping an octave, making Ryan feel all girlie inside.

"Thank you for the flowers. They're amazing."

"You're welcome."

"Even if you had them delivered earlier than the bird that got the worm."

"Ha!"

"Just kidding. It was very thoughtful of you. I appreciate it."

"There were two reasons why I had them delivered now. One, in case you had plans they could arrive before you left home. Two, if you don't have plans, you could join me here, at the ranch. I'm going riding in an hour and would love for you to join me."

"What kind of riding?" Ryan purposely asked the question in a way that could hold many meanings, as though she hadn't told herself just moments ago that the two had no future together. Her willpower had been strong, her decision firm. And then she'd heard that sexy voice. Dammit.

"There's certain types of riding I welcome at any time." Ryan smiled at the inflections in Adam's voice, leaving no doubt as to what kind of riding he meant. "But right now," he continued, "I meant horse riding. It occurred to me that I'd never invited you out for one of my favorite pastimes."

"Horse riding. That sounds so…highbrow."

"That's probably because of the cost of maintaining horses, which can be expensive. But spending time with, taking care of and bonding with horses is one of the best experiences any human being could have, and there are ways for anyone to enjoy that, no matter their social or economic status."

"They're beautiful animals."

"Have you never ridden a horse before?"

"Never."

"I'll send a car over and you'll see that it's the perfect way to start the day."

"Just text the address instead. I'd rather have my car to run errands afterward."

An hour later, Ryan pulled her car up to the grand wrought iron entrance. A friendly-looking gentleman came out of the guardhouse located just outside the gate. She looked around at the picturesque scene and tried to imagine actually living here. She couldn't.

"Good afternoon, Ms. Washington," the guard said.

Ryan didn't try to hide her surprise. "How do you know my name?"

"Adam informed me of your imminent arrival and my need to provide directions for you to get to his ranch."

He handed her a square white card that contained a map of the estate. She could see where a pen had been taken to highlight the route to Adam's house.

"It's a lot of land and can feel intimidating, but if you head straight down this road, all the way, then take a left here, and a right by the pond, you'll see the arch for Breedlove Ranch. Can't miss it from there."

"Thank you."

Ryan entered the estate, her eyes widening as they took in the sheer beauty of the land. The grass was the most uniform shade of green she'd seen outside of Astroturf. *Pristine* didn't begin to describe her surroundings. She didn't see a speck of dirt out of place, an errant leaf on the ground. And were those peacocks? Her jaw dropped.

Ryan was emotional by nature and by the time she reached Adam's spread, the estate's beauty had almost brought tears. She drove under the arch and down to where she saw Adam looking like a cowboy ad again, his booted foot on a plank of fence, a kerchief around his neck. Beyond him, two horses trotted in a corral. Farther away, cows dotted the landscape. Seeing them sobered her a bit. They were leisurely grazing when she knew how their story would end.

As she pulled in, Adam walked over. "Hello."

"This place is amazing," Ryan said, as they hugged. "The other night I could feel that the area was vast, but to see it in the daytime? Wow."

"Did you have any trouble finding me?"

"No, but only because I had a map, the first time needing one after arriving at my destination."

Adam smiled, stepped back and whistled. "Whoa, girl. Look at you wearing those jeans!"

He reached out and felt the denim. "The material is a bit thin, though. I hope they'll be okay."

"We're riding horses, right, not bucking broncos?"

"Ha! I guess you've got a point." He checked out her sneakers. "These will do for today but we're going to have to get you a pair of boots."

"Anything else, fashion stylist?"

He gave her a once-over that warmed her blood. "That's all for now. Come on, so I can introduce you to Biscuit."

The horse was beautiful, the landscape breathtaking, the riding easy. Ryan enjoyed it more than she'd imagined. Back at the house Adam's actions made it clear that he was interested in a different kind of ride. An afternoon of lovemaking was tempting. Adam's sexual prowess would have been the perfect birthday present. But doing so would have only prolonged the inevitable.

She eased herself from Adam's embrace and took a few steps to put distance between them before turning around.

"There's no denying our sexual compatibility. You are totally intoxicating."

Adam walked over to a chair and sat down. "I think I hear a 'but' coming."

"But…" Ryan smiled as she sat on an opposite chair. "This is a very busy time for both of us. I'm getting my practice ready to open and next week you'll be orienting a new employee—my brother."

"Does his moving here bother you? Or is it that he'll be working for me?"

"A little bit of both, but mainly it's that you and I agreed that our getting together would be fun, casual and uncomplicated. I'm not sure that by continuing to see you it can stay that way."

As the words left Ryan's mouth she felt her heart ache. The slight narrowing of Adam's eyes showed they'd affected him, too. But when he spoke, his tone was casual.

"Are you starting to have feelings for me?"

"You're a good man, Adam, very easy to like, and yes, I could probably fall in love with you. Right guy, wrong timing, for many reasons. None of them personal. Maybe later on we can hook up again, after both our new ventures are off the ground and life has calmed down. I'd like that…very much."

He looked at her a long moment, then walked over and tugged her out of the chair. "I don't think I've ever been dumped so eloquently," he said, pulling her into an embrace. "But you've got to do what you've got to do, baby. It sounds as though you've already made your decision so of course I'll support it, and you. Good luck with your business."

"Thanks, you too," Ryan said, swallowing the cry that clawed at her throat, blinking back the tears that threatened. She ended their embrace and tried to lighten the moment. "With my brother working for you I'm sure I'll see you around. When that happens, behave yourself," she playfully chided. "No undressing me with your eyes or giving me that sexy look that will have me wanting to take my own clothes off."

"I promise nothing," he said, punctuating the statement with a look that was as sexy as hell.

"You're incorrigible," she said, gathering her things.

"Thank you." They laughed. "You sure you don't want to stay for a late lunch or early dinner?"

"Positive. I need to leave before this very tenuous resolve I feel totally melts away. Oh, I'll send you some information on handling dyslexia. I did a bit of research and think you'll find it as interesting as I did."

"Sure, send it over. I've overcome it for the most part, except when I'm frustrated or rattled. But I'm open to reading what you found."

"For frustration and anxieties, deep breathing works wonders. It's something few people do, fill the lungs with air that expands the stomach so that the oxygen can circulate, stimulate the organs and the body."

"I can think of an organ and how it can be used for stimulation."

"On that note…" Said with a smile as she shouldered her tote and walked outside.

Adam walked her to her car, opened the door and placed a light kiss on her forehead.

"Stay gorgeous," he said.

"Stay handsome," she replied. "I'll see you around."

She kept the smile in place until she'd exited the estate's wrought iron gates. Then her eyes teared up again. She missed Adam already.

Eleven

Adam hadn't wanted to stop seeing Ryan romantically, but he didn't dwell on it. There was simply no time. With the construction for CANN Island underway, he had the freedom to focus more fully on Breedlove Beef Processing Center. The state-of-the-art facility had been erected near the far north end of Breedlove property, downwind from the closest residents and miles away from where the cattle were bred and raised. The exterior of the four-thousand-square-foot building was made of brick, wood and aluminum. The interior was a wonder in those elements combined with stainless steel. Adam knew architecture and construction. Dennis knew meat-processing plants. It had made for a winning combination in creating a facility that at best rivaled and would likely far exceed any other facility in the country.

The first Wagyu shipments were scheduled for the second week in December. Dennis suggested the meat be allowed to age for three to four weeks. So the first butchering had been scheduled to happen next week. Adam was both excited and nervous. It would be his ranch's first time handling the process from beginning to end. For the past half hour he and Dennis had been in the field, marking cattle for market. Now Adam headed back to meet the workers Dennis had hired and make sure his precise instructions had been conveyed and would be followed.

He pulled a rugged Jeep into a temporary gravel-strewn parking lot. Adam exited on one side while Dennis hopped out of the other. Dozens of men milled around outside, finishing stalls, walkways and other tasks. Adam saw the foreman talking with a group. Rather than interrupt him he simply waved before he and Dennis stepped inside the space.

Dennis placed his hands on his hips and took in the vast interior. "Man, I tell you what. This is a long way from the geodesic dome I built in the backyard."

Adam looked at him. "The what?"

"You never saw my dome? Oh, that's right. You never came over."

"I don't remember ever being invited. Had that happened, I probably would have accepted and come over. Especially if I'd known you were building something. That's been a passion of mine from the time I was a little boy. That and horses, or anything to do with a ranch."

"I remember that side of you well, your love for horses and horsepower, like that souped-up '65 Chevy you owned."

Adam laughed. "Ah, that was my baby. Belonged to my grandfather. We still have it."

"I'd love to see it again. That was a pretty ride. A rich kid who had everything. To me, that was you."

"Maybe, but life wasn't perfect, remember? That's how we met."

Dennis clapped Adam on the back. "Nobody's perfect, brother. At least you have an excuse for difficulty reading. I can read fine, just hate to do it."

"Why?"

Dennis shrugged. "Never was into the books much. Even now, I only read when necessary. Otherwise I'd rather be doing something with my hands or outside."

"I can understand that."

They stopped in front of a large enclosed space. Dennis stood next to Adam. "Does Ryan know about your... problem?"

Adam frowned, remembering he'd told her and wishing he hadn't, even though there wasn't another human on the planet who could have been more understanding, and even though he'd largely conquered the condition. "Yes."

"Just asking," Dennis said, his hands raised in apology.

"Don't worry about it. Defense mechanism." Adam began walking the periphery of the main floor. Dennis followed suit. "After being properly diagnosed, I was given tools to counteract the effects of dyslexia—the use of phonics, color codes, exercises in how to focus. Ryan emailed me a few natural remedies. Kinda cool what she does, healing various ailments through natural means."

"A bunch of hocus-pocus if you ask me," Dennis said. Then after a beat, "Are you and my sister dating?"

"We're friends," Adam said.

"With benefits?"

Adam's pause in movement and barely raised eyebrow was the only physical reaction to Dennis's inappropriate question. "Friends, period."

They stepped onto a rectangular-shaped area of the concrete floor. Dennis wisely changed the subject.

"This holding pen came out real nice," he said.

"It's called a lairage," Adam corrected.

"Maybe," Dennis responded. "But in lay terms it's a pen that holds animals, so that's what I call it—a holding pen."

The humor melted the frostiness that Dennis's comment had created. "Where are the guys?" Adam asked.

"In the main conference room, boss, waiting for you."

"Let's get this party started." Adam headed toward the stairs, confident that he'd chosen the right man to bring his dreams into reality.

Today was a big one for Adam. In mid-November, after five years of planning, three years of implementing those plans and almost a year of working with a PR and marketing team to brand the company as one dealing with only the most exclusive members of the hospitality industry, Breedlove Wagyu was being unveiled. It had been a long and hard road with a steep learning curve. But in the process of acting as both boss and eager student, the makings of an empire had come together—assembling a meatpacking industry dream team, acquiring livestock, monitoring intake for maximum quality, building the processing plant, and securing national and international customers to enjoy the fruits of their labor.

The black-tie event he'd planned would take place at the CANN Casino Hotel and Spa and give two hundred people from all over the world a taste of the meticulously prepared meat. As often happened when attending an event there, Adam was staying in one of three deluxe suites that were used almost exclusively by the Breedlove family. Ryan had spent the previous night there, too. They hadn't seen each other since that day at the ranch, but they'd kept in touch. Without the physical distraction, each had learned greater aspects of the other. Their friendship deepened. When he asked if she'd escort him to the dinner, she'd said yes without hesitation. When he shared plans to spend a few days at the hotel in his private suite and asked if she'd join him, she'd hesitated only briefly before saying yes to that, too.

"I've missed your stimulating organ," she'd told him.

"I've missed everything about you," he'd honestly replied.

Adam had surprised Ryan by having a gown delivered, one he said had been customized just for her. Again, she'd been moved by his attention to detail. Meticulous not only in business, but in his personal life as well. She'd argued the gift was too extravagant, had thought the chiffon dress she'd purchased from a designer outlet store had been a steal of a deal. But once she'd stepped into Adam's gift there was no comparison. The stretchy silk fabric caressed her body, had structure while at the same time being flowy and light. The color was that of a deep burgundy wine with colorful crystals—the name of which Ryan didn't remember and couldn't pronounce—splashed as though tossed across the bodice and down a skirt that draped into a short train. When she looked in the mirror, she hardly recognized the woman who looked back at her.

Adam had gone for simple and classic. A tailored black tuxedo had been paired with a white shirt, striped vest and black tie, his black suede shoes the only nod to his understated fashion sense. As he looked in the mirror, he felt hands run up his back and squeeze his shoulders before Ryan came from behind him and looked at his mirror image.

"You look hot, guy."

"Thank you, gorgeous." He ran a hand over soft curls that glistened slightly thanks to the hairdresser who'd styled him less than an hour ago. He turned to face her, admiring the Grecian-styled burgundy number with crystals haphazardly splashed from head to toe. "You… look amazing. I love your hair like that."

"Yes, well, take a picture, because any style that takes longer than ten minutes is one I won't wear much."

Adam fingered the thick tresses that had been flat-ironed and now flowed over her shoulders.

"So…what's our story?" she asked.

"Story?"

"We're attending a high-profile dinner together, one that I imagine will be covered by the press. Dennis will be there and he already suspects we're seeing each other. So when people ask, what is our story?"

"You are a beautiful woman, a vegetarian friend who graciously accepted my invitation to a dinner serving tons of meat. To me, that makes you a very accommodating friend and a superspecial date."

"People will assume we're dating."

Adam placed a gentle kiss on Ryan's temple and whispered in her ear. "Take a deep breath, darling, and don't worry about it. Worse assumptions could be made."

He placed his hand at the small of her back, letting it slide to the low vee cut of the dress, then lower, to her butt. They exited the suite and crossed the hall to the elevator. "You sure you'll be all right surrounded by plates of premium beef?"

The elevator doors opened. They stepped in. Ryan moved close to Adam and pressed her body to his. "This will be enough premium beef to distract me," she cooed, squeezing his Grade A rump. Adam lowered his lips to hers, searing her with a kiss that lasted one hundred floors.

Even before reaching one of the hotel's smaller ball-rooms, a buzz of excitement was heard. Ryan watched as Adam squared his shoulders—unconsciously, she thought—and entered the room with a confident swagger that seemed etched into a Breedlove's DNA. Immediately, they were the center of attention. Or Adam was, to be more precise. Reporters, clients, well-wishers, women, all moved toward him as if drawn by a magnet. The more assertive females seemed to have little regard for Ryan as they tried to maneuver past her to be by his side. Ever aware, Adam reached for Ryan's hand and held it tightly as he engaged those close enough to speak or ask questions while navigating his way to the front of the room and the Breedlove table. The gesture made her feel protected. Clearly, of all of the men in the room, she was with the prize.

They slowed as they reached the table directly be-hind the one where Adam's family sat. Ryan saw Den-nis, looking fresh and clean-shaven, all gussied up for the occasion. He stood to speak to them. Ryan didn't see her brother dressed up often. She thought he looked quite the executive in a double-breasted navy suit. She couldn't say the same for the snake beside him. Of all the people who could have been his plus-one, why'd her brother bring Luke?

Dennis had barely finished speaking before Luke

thrust out his hand. He spoke to Adam but was drinking in Ryan as though she was the last glass of water in the Mojave Desert.

"Good to see you again, Adam. You, too, Ryan. You're looking good." He held out his arm for a handshake. Adam shifted Ryan away from him. If that move didn't tell Luke that she was off-limits, his barely concealed scowl surely did.

Ryan remained quiet and suppressed a smile. *Oh those alpha males!*

Luke dropped his hand and cleared this throat. "Um, Dennis has been bragging about the beef you raised. Wish I could have been a part of that process but…I'm looking forward to dinner."

"Dennis spoke very highly of you," Adam said. Ryan felt Adam was leery of Luke and thought his was a diplomatic answer that allowed his opinions to be kept to himself.

"Rusty, there—" He nodded at an older gentleman whose tanned, weathered face told a story that included years in the sun. "He's been with the family a long time, is an expert on animals and already worked at the ranch. Whenever possible, we like to promote from within. So that's what we did."

"That's an excellent thing to do for your employees," Luke replied. "I just met Mr. O'Brien. Great guy. But I told Dennis to let me know if an opening comes up. I could use a change of scenery and I think the Vegas lifestyle might work."

Or not, thought Ryan.

Adam said nothing, just gave a slight head nod and continued to the next table, where his family sat. His chagrin with Luke was palpable. Ryan gave his forearm an affectionate squeeze and heard him exhale. *Relax.*

"There's the man of the hour!" Christian stood and gave his brother a hearty hug while Nick and Noah chatted with Ryan.

"Babe." Adam pulled her closer to him. "This is my older brother, Christian, and his wife, Lauren. She's the good taste behind that dress you love."

"Oh my goodness, you picked this out?" Ryan leaned down to give Lauren a hug. "It's beautiful."

"Looks like it was made for you," Lauren said. "The way that color highlights your skin...fabulous!"

"Thank you. That's a wonderful color you're wearing. Are you a model?"

Lauren laughed. "Hardly."

Christian heard the comment as he sat down beside her. "See, babe, I told you. You could be."

Lauren shook her head.

"You really could be. That color is very complementary. What is it, like a..."

"Emerald green," Lauren said. "Christian's favorite color for me to wear, right, babe?"

"No," Christian said, lowering his voice so that only Lauren and Ryan could hear. "My favorite color on you is nude."

Lauren gave him a playful swat. "You're so bad."

Christian kissed her cheek. "That's why you love me."

Adam introduced Ryan to the others at the table she'd not yet met. When meeting his grandmother Jewel and stepgrandfather Will Breedlove, he reminded her that while out horseback riding, their home was the one they had seen with the imposing cedar arch whose inscription announced La Hacienda Breedlove. He introduced Lauren's parents and told her that Lauren's father also worked for CANN International. Once they sat down,

Adam explained that he would have introduced Noah's and Nick's dates, had he known their names.

"Until those two," Adam continued in a whisper, "I thought Christian was the ultimate playboy. These guys took playing the field to a whole other level. They built a whole new stadium for their game."

The evening began. Ryan found herself enjoying what she thought would be a drudge to get through. Though identical, she quickly learned one way the twins were different. Noah was quiet. Nick was a hoot. Five minutes in and it felt as though she'd known him forever and easily imagined him the irksome younger brother that Adam described.

A venerable army of waiters began serving courses with an equally proficient group of bussers quickly clearing the used china after each one. Ryan watched the orchestration in awe. The first course, a chilled vegan soup, was exquisite.

The table made quick work of the second course. The bussers appeared from several entrances to do their thing. She picked up her glass of tea and sat back to watch them, to admire their efficiency and ability to move around bone china while hardly making a sound. As a group neared her table she locked eyes with a woman who was…no…it couldn't be…her birth mother, Phyllis.

"Are you all right?"

Adam's voice pierced through Ryan's shock. Only then did she realize her hand gripped his forearm. The woman faced her fully, her features better lit under the table's light. She could have been her mother's twin, but it wasn't her.

"Oh, sorry. I, um…" She eased her hand from Adam's

arm, her voice trailing off as well. "It's nothing," she finally managed.

"Are you sure, baby?" Ryan's eyes pierced her, filled with concern. "You look like you've seen a ghost."

Ryan shook her head, further rattled by the accurate assessment Adam's common phrase delivered.

"It was work, something I thought I forgot," she said, giving him the first answer she thought he'd find plausible. "But I didn't. It's okay."

Finally assuaged, Adam's attention turned elsewhere.

The evening continued. So did the queasy feeling in the pit of her stomach, along with the questions her reaction brought up. Why had the thought of seeing her mother caused so much angst? If discovered, how would Adam and his family respond to her past, the drug addiction and jail time? Ryan had wanted nothing more than to get to know her birth mother. She hadn't considered how that relationship might impact other parts of her life. Ryan felt burdened by the weight of her secrets, and the fear that Sin City wasn't big enough to hold them all.

Twelve

That Sunday, the day after the Breedlove Beef official unveiling, Ryan pulled up a website on her computer, one that she hoped might help her find her birth dad. Her reaction last night to seeing the woman who looked like Phyllis had been surprising and left her shaken. She'd always longed for a relationship with her mother, but had never given much thought to what that would look like, how Phyllis's presence might impact other areas of her life. She was, after all, basically a stranger. Who was she beyond the woman who'd given her life? And equally as important, who was her father?

Ryan had nothing, not even a name, to begin the search. That week, while working with Brooklyn to put the final touches on their office, Ryan shared "a client's" frustration of not being able to trace her ancestry. Brooklyn told her about a show she'd seen on television where birth parents of adopted children were found through matching DNA that had been placed in a national database. The odds weren't in Ryan's favor. Any potential blood relative out there would have to be in that system, also looking for lost family. It was a long shot but the only one that Ryan had. She pulled out a credit card and ordered the kit. That done, she switched her focus from personal to business. The day she and Brooklyn had dreamed of had almost arrived. The next day Integrative Healing opened for business. The whirlwind began.

The first week wasn't jam-packed with clients but Ryan and Brooklyn were busy. If either had free time during the day, they'd market online, network with other practitioners through cross-promotions and referrals, and one day hit the Strip and Fremont Street downtown with their mobile chairs, offering neck and shoulder massages. By the end of that first week both women were stressed, and asking each other what the heck had they been thinking, to which Brooklyn's spiritual adviser said, "Awesome! Sounds like you're exactly where you need to be!"

Ryan left her office and went to the break room. Brooklyn was pouring herself a drink from a glass pitcher.

"Sit down, girl, relax for a minute. I'm serving us up some celebratory kombucha."

Ryan leaned on the counter where Brooklyn worked. "I've been sitting for the past two hours. Think I'm going to hit a yoga class before I go home."

She took the tumbler that Brooklyn offered, and clinked the thick glass against the other. "What are we toasting exactly?"

"One week in business, and neither one of us died."

"Ha! And we're still friends," Ryan added.

"And Johnny still loves me even though all week I've been too tired to make love. Heck, I couldn't even make like."

Ryan and Brooklyn cracked up laughing. "We're delirious," Brooklyn finally decided.

Ryan nodded. "Yeah, it feels good to laugh."

"Your energy definitely feels better now than it did on Monday. I knew something was going on but I didn't want to ask—figured you'd tell me when you're ready."

Ryan nodded. "I will."

"I was kind of hoping the good mood had to do with Adam."

Ryan's smile disappeared.

"Did something happen?"

"Not really," she said finally. "And nothing ever will. He's a fun date, but it's about time to pull the plug on that fantasy."

"It's obvious how much you like him. Why would you end something making you happy?"

"Why prolong the inevitable? It's only a matter of time before he ditches the person he likes to sleep around with for someone he can marry."

"Don't underestimate your value, Ryan Washington. If anything serious happens between you and Adam, he will be the lucky one."

Thanksgiving arrived, giving Ryan a much-needed break from work. Word of mouth helped the clientele grow quickly for her, Brooklyn and the acupuncturist Suyin. The personal front wasn't running as smoothly. Feeling her life was already filled with too many secrets, she finally told Ida that she'd reconnected with Phyllis and that she hoped to find her birth father, too.

Ida called it a betrayal. Her usually supportive father

had sided with Ida and told Ryan she shouldn't have "done this behind your mother's back." Though their reaction was painful, Ryan was glad to have her search out in the open. Now all she could do was wait for the DNA results that would hopefully lead to information on her father's family.

The only bright spot was Adam. Their called-off liaison was on again. They'd only seen each other a couple more times, but oh those memorable nights. She was falling in love with him. A problem, but right now his touch wasn't a luxury. It was a necessity that helped keep her sane. When he suggested she spend Thanksgiving at the estate, and to invite her family, Ryan initially said no. But asking her mother what she thought about the prospect of spending the holiday in Vegas with the owners of CANN melted the chill and got them talking again. Ryan was optimistic that this visit would go well. Ugly attitudes had no place in a setting as beautiful as that of the Breedlove estate.

On Thursday, the weather couldn't have been more perfect. A bit chilly, but as Ryan reached the tents that had been erected for today's dinner, she saw the strategically placed heaters that would keep everyone toasty and warm. She knew her family was already there and she spotted them right away. She waved and headed over. Everyone was all smiles. Her father's deteriorating health was a continuing concern but today he managed to look dapper in dress slacks and a sweater over a shirt and tie. For the first time since Ryan could remember lately, her mom had curls! Dennis's look was more casual but Ryan saw that he'd still not regrown his beard. She didn't know the woman sitting beside him.

"Hey, everybody!" Starting with her father, she greeted everyone.

Soon, Victoria joined them. "Hello, Ryan!" They shared a warm embrace.

"You've met my mom and dad?"

"I have and it's such a pleasure. Adam believes that Dennis is a solid addition to the team. You remember Lauren, of course."

"Of course! Hi, Lauren."

"Hey, Ryan." The women shared a brief hug. "It's good seeing you again. I heard about your new business for holistic health. Congratulations."

"Thanks, Lauren."

"I'd love to know more about it. In fact, I have a quick question. Never mind. It's a holiday and listen to me putting you right to work."

Ryan laughed. "I don't mind."

Lauren and Ryan stepped away from the others. The conversation began with Lauren's interest in acupuncture, then turned to Ryan and Adam.

"You guys look like you belong together. You make a nice couple."

"Me and Adam?" Ryan asked. "We're just friends."

Lauren laughed as though Ryan had just told a joke. "I saw how that man looks at you, with love in his eyes. The way yours lit up at that statement, I'd say the feeling was mutual."

"I might be falling in love a little," Ryan admitted. It felt good to say it out loud. The more time she spent with Adam, the more she found to love about him. Perhaps it was time for another conversation, for what they shared to be redefined.

"I'll admit to being surprised when he told me about you. I love your vibe, but never thought I'd see any of the brothers with someone with such an earthiness and realness about them. Of course," she continued,

"I never thought they'd have looked twice at someone like me, either. So I hope you don't take what I'm saying the wrong way."

"Not at all. I would totally put them with a model/celebrity type." Ryan nodded toward the twins. "Like the women Noah and Nick brought with them."

Lauren eyed their dates. "Those guys are having so much fun right now. They love being with women who are drop-dead gorgeous, and who fawn all over them as though they're God's gift to heaven. But trust me, those feelings don't run too deep. They've been well-schooled by their older brothers on what type of women to watch out for, and the myriad of ways a woman can scheme to get into their wallet."

Ryan and Lauren continued to watch the women with the twins. They were stunningly gorgeous, no doubt about that, with bodies that could have been bought and paid for. If so, it was money well spent. She smiled, but inside couldn't help feeling that if Adam knew about her background he might believe that she was on the "come up," too.

The day was lovely. Ryan appreciated the attention Victoria paid to her family, making sure they felt welcomed. Common ground was found between Victoria and Ida when she mentioned the CANN Foundation, and the fund-raising done for various charities. Victoria promised to invite her to a future event. Ryan could tell that made her mom happy. Both she and her mom were surprised to learn that the delicious meal—turkey, Wagyu beef and tons of sides—had all been prepared by the family's matriarch, Adam's grandmother Jewel, with assistance from several family members. Adam joined her at the table with her mother and dad, while

Dennis sat with guys from the processing plant and his date, a woman Ida told Ryan he'd met online.

Just before dessert was set to be served, Ryan made a quick trip to the restroom. She returned and was surprised to see Dennis halfway up the walk assisting their father, and Ida making apologies for their unexpected and abrupt departure.

"What's happening, Mom?"

"Your father's not feeling well. We're going to take him back to the hotel where he can rest."

"I'll meet you there."

"There's no need for that, Ryan. Dennis will be close by if we need him, and all your father is going to do is sleep."

Adam came up then and placed an arm around Ryan's shoulders. "Is everything okay?"

"It's my dad. I could tell how much he enjoyed himself today but I think he may have overdone it a bit." She turned to Ida. "I'm going to meet you at the hotel, Mom."

"Okay."

After talking Adam out of coming with her, and taking the containers filled with desserts as Victoria insisted, Ryan left the estate and headed toward downtown Las Vegas and Fremont Street, where her parents were staying. She worked a variety of healing modalities on her dad and left him sleeping peacefully, with Dennis and his girlfriend in a room down the hall. She spent the night with Adam. Her parents had planned to stay the weekend but her father continued to feel bad so they left the next day.

Two days later, her father passed out and was rushed to the hospital by ambulance. Tests were run. The news was not good. His kidneys were no longer functioning. Only intense dialysis or a kidney transplant would keep him alive.

Thirteen

For the past several days, Ryan had been Adam's priority. Hearing her father's prognosis had been understandably upsetting. He'd offered his many resources to help. Walking into the boardroom at CANN International, Adam was prepared to provide updates on the various stages of design and construction happening with half a dozen new CANN hotels going up in the next eighteen months. Along with CANN Island, an ambitious string of über-luxurious properties on islands near Djibouti, plans were underway for hotels in Geneva, Sydney, Fiji, Oslo and Macao.

No one was talking about that. The chatter was all about Wagyu.

As soon as Adam reached the table his dad, Nicholas, exclaimed, "Breedlove Beef is king!"

"Oh, here we go," Adam said, though he couldn't

help but for his chest to puff out just a bit. He accepted several handshakes before sitting down.

Greg Chapman, VP of international sales, agreed with Nicholas. "You're all the industry is talking about."

"The money spent on public relations paid off, and it was a boatload. No doubt the column written by one of America's top food critics—"

"And published in the Sunday edition of every major city—"

"Right," Adam said. "There really isn't a dollar amount that can be put on that."

"I bet they tried, though," Christian added, holding up a fist for Adam to bump.

"No doubt. The retainer is hefty, plus expenses. But the phone has been ringing off the hook. We might have to cut back some of those orders for…"

Nicholas sat up. "Orders for who? I know you're not going to say the orders for CANN International, the other company you work for, the reason you even have your little enterprise." Nicholas's dismissive wave of the hand elicited laughter around the table. "I know that's not the company you're planning to put on the end of that sentence. The first shipments of that prime, in-demand Wagyu need to be addressed to CANN International, and that's after you've come up the road and filled up my and your mama's fridge."

The jokes continued for a bit before Christian took charge and returned their attention to CANN business. It was like each brother had been born with a specific talent that together could create one's empire of choice, all overseen by their father, the ultimate dreamer. Christian was company president. Adam handled expansion as the R&D VP. Noah worked in finance. Numbers came to him the way music came to Mozart. His family teased that instead of asking for video games, Noah wanted calculators. He was quiet, introspective and smart as a whip. Which left Nick, the patriarch's namesake. The most charismatic and carefree one of the bunch, he was officially a member of the sales force, but someone with Nick's personality could basically be successful doing whatever he wanted.

Once everyone had their say the meeting ended. The brothers hung back while the others returned to their offices. The next thing anyone knew, Adam was being hit in the head with a Nerf football that Nick found God knows where.

"Hey!" Adam reached for the ball and aimed for the brother now using the table as a shield. Adam fired as hard as one could a Nerf ball, missing his brother's head by inches. "Fool."

"When am I going to get some of that good beef?" Nick asked.

"What do you mean? You've tasted it several times."

"I'm talking about a stash for the house, like Dad was saying."

"Nick's right," Noah chimed in. "A couple rib eyes would be nice."

"Y'all are a trip," Adam said, laughing along with his brothers as they left the conference room and went back to their offices while he headed out of the building. With the meetings over for the day, it was time to go to the ranch. On the way he remembered something Noah had said after being introduced to Ryan's family.

"I hope that guy Dennis works out for you, bro. If you fire her brother, I'm not sure Ryan will stick around."

He'd been joking, of course. But when Noah asked, Adam hadn't denied that Dennis's relationship to Ryan had given him an edge over the competition. Still, there was a matter Adam wanted to revisit.

He rounded the corner to find the new manager standing just outside the small meeting room, looking over the balustrade that allowed a full view of the barn floor below, where long rectangular tables held a variety of equipment and devices used on the ranch. Rows of grain, also cow feed, went on for several acres. A pond could be seen from the second floor, along with cows roaming freely over the hills. Adam frowned, not because Dennis was standing around not working, but because of who was beside him, someone who as far as Adam was concerned had no business here.

Dennis heard Adam's boots on the floor and turned. "Adam! Hey, buddy. We were just talking about you."

Adam reached him. He and Dennis shook hands.

"Man, this place is awesome," Luke said, his arm outstretched.

Adam was slow to shake it.

"I hope you don't mind that I'm showing Luke the building. He was in town and asked for a tour, was curious about how operating an organic process differed from how it's done at Bakersfield."

"That's part of it," Luke added. "The other is that I'd really like to work here. Everything's fine at Bakersfield Meat and I never thought the word *beautiful* could describe a slaughterhouse, but this place is amazing. Working for Breedlove Beef would definitely be a step up." He added a chuckle as though he were joking, but Adam got the feeling that he meant every word.

"I told Luke about coming over here back in the day. Even then, being at the estate felt like I was visiting royalty—"

"Yeah, right."

"You know it was like that. Saturday mornings, Sunday afternoon, this was the place to be! It was cool then, but the way you've turned this side of the estate into a cow ranch beyond the best I've ever seen...well, it's impressive."

"I appreciate that," Adam said. "Especially with the hands-on experience you have in the industry. Luke, Dennis and I need to meet. Is there anything Olivia could get for you? Coffee, soda, a beer, before you're on your way?"

"No, I'm fine. I need to get downtown and handle a few things myself." Luke craned his neck before his eyes settled on the petite older woman sitting at a desk at the end of the hall. "That your full-time secretary?"

"Olivia? Secretary, teacher, mother figure, boss. I've known her my whole life. Her husband, Clarence, passed at about the same time I started building this place. I thought taking care of things around here would give her something else to focus on besides how lonely life was without him."

"You're a good man, Adam," Dennis said.

"I try." When he saw Luke still standing beside them, he looked over to where one of the workers was cleaning a stall. "Hey, Bobby. Do me a favor and escort our visitor to the gate."

Dennis mumbled a goodbye and followed Adam toward the meeting room. Luke walked outside with the worker, clearly dismissed.

"Hope you don't mind that I showed Luke around," Dennis said as they settled into chairs in the meeting room with a large window through which cows could be seen grazing at their leisure.

"For someone who says he's fine at his present job, he seems eager to try out a new one."

"That's probably my fault," Dennis said. "I've bragged about this operation since day one. He's seen all of the positive write-ups about the company. Heck, everybody has seen them. He knows what a fun town Vegas can be. Housing prices beat those in California hands down. There's no state tax. Lots of beautiful women. Luke's a bit of a hardhead but overall a good dude."

"Would Ryan agree with you?" Adam paid close attention to Dennis's reaction, saw a flash of annoyance before Dennis schooled his features.

"Probably not," Dennis said with a bit of a chuckle. "Luke used to tease Ryan. She didn't like it. Too sensitive. He used to flirt with her, even though it was clear she didn't like bad boys, which is what she considered him back then."

"Was he?"

Dennis shrugged. "He got into a little trouble, a run-in or two with the law. But that was a long time ago, Adam. Like me, Luke's changed. We've all grown up."

Dennis's frank answer was unexpected and basically lined up with what Ryan had alluded to when he'd asked her about Luke.

"One more thing. You resigned in Bakersfield before I hired you. Why?"

"It was foolhardy, I know. But I was beginning to have problems with one of the owners, issues about safety, and pay. I should have told you, Adam, but I wanted the job and knew I could do it."

"You're proving that and yes, resigning is something you should have disclosed. Thanks for being honest." Adam stood, satisfied that he'd made the right choice. "I have to go to a meeting."

He headed home, where Ryan would meet him for

a trip to BBs and a sampling of the new vegetarian options. Later that night, despite their resolve, they spent a leisurely hour sampling each other.

Fourteen

The Christmas season was Ryan's favorite time of the year. She loved everything about the holiday—crisp winter weather, colorful decorations, shopping, singing, everyone filled with cheer. As she headed to Bakersfield, her thoughts were on Joe, her adoptive dad. The dialysis wasn't working. He needed a kidney transplant. The immediate family was being tested, along with Joe's brother and nephew. Because being a blood relative wasn't a mandatory requirement when seeking a potential donor, Ryan would be tested, too. Joe had always treated her the same as he treated Dennis. Like his very own child. For him to live, she'd give up her kidney in a heartbeat.

Holiday traffic was heavy. Ryan arrived at her parents' just after dark. Christmas lights outlined the house. The same artificial tree with white lights and gold bulbs that had graced the living room for at least the past decade could be seen through the window. Ryan pulled her luggage from the trunk and reached into the back seat for her Christmas gifts. As she started up the walk the door opened. Her mother came out, not quite smiling, but with a look that came close.

"Hi, Ryan."

"Hey, Mom. Merry Christmas!"

"Not for another few hours. Do you need help?"

Ida met her halfway and took the shopping bag filled with presents. At Thanksgiving dinner, Ryan had told Ida what happened with her birth mother and didn't miss the irony that her falling-out with Phyllis had further thawed Ida's demeanor. She stepped inside, stopped, inhaled and was transported to her preteen years. The smell of mulled tea blended with that of the crispy sugar cookies. During the twelve days of Christmas and Kwanzaa the cookie jar would be kept full, guaranteed. When she turned the corner, took in the familiar tree with the kente-clothed angel topper, the dining room centerpiece she'd helped pick out, and other decorations she used to help hang with family and some of the neighborhood friends, Ryan was surprised to feel love swell up inside. It had been a while since she'd felt this way but tonight, it felt good to be home.

Ryan greeted her father, then made a beeline for the cookie jar. "Where's Dennis? I thought he'd be here by now."

"Oh, he's here. So is April."

"April? Where's Ginny, the girl from Thanksgiving?"

Ida shrugged. "Turned out to be a turkey, I guess."

Ryan laughed out loud, both shocked and delighted at Ida's joke. She didn't make them often.

April had lived next door with her parents and siblings when the Washingtons moved there. She was a cute girl, on the thick side, with expressive eyes and a hearty laugh. Dennis always denied they were in a relationship, but Ryan had seen him tiptoe across the backyard more than once. He'd gone into the service and when he came back April was married. But Ida had never been convinced that the two stopped hooking up.

"Divorced and back home with two kids. She was real happy to see your brother." Ida stopped and looked over her reading glasses with an expression that conveyed "you know what I mean."

The neighbors came over. One of her dad's good friends and former postal coworkers stopped by with another type of cheer, a brown liquor in a blue pouch that made the men jolly, and after mixing theirs with cola had the women's spirits bright, too. When a random scrolling through the channels revealed a harried Jimmy Stewart feeling trapped in his life, the room settled into watching the black-and-white classic. Perfect entertainment and a feel-good finish. Even with the challenges ahead, it felt like a wonderful life!

Ryan went to bed when the movie ended. She woke up hours later to a dark room, a quiet house, a mouth filled with cotton and a vow to never drink strong liquor again. She headed downstairs for a glass of water, added a smaller glass of juice and a bag of chips to the mix, and tiptoed back upstairs.

Passing Dennis's room, she heard voices. Ryan's eyes widened. April? No! Ryan hurried to her room, deposited her midnight kitchen run and tiptoed back ever so quietly to her brother's door. What was happening in Dennis's room was none of her business. But Ryan couldn't resist. Cupping her hand, she placed it against the door with her ear firm against it. She heard Dennis's voice first.

"The money is rolling in like water, man, two hundred and fifty a pound."

Ryan thought her brother could use a brushup on his pillow talk but maybe April was a meat lover. Could be sexy.

"I'm telling you, man. We could get in on that."

Not April's voice…at all.

"I just started working there, dude. I'm not trying to risk my job like that."

"It wouldn't be a risk. You're in charge! I've got the substitute."

Dennis was talking on his cell phone, with Luke's voice coming through the speaker loud and clear. The conversation was making her stomach roil again.

"You said it yourself—there are thousands of pounds. You think with all that shipping going on they'll catch a few swapped-out steaks here and there? Going all over the world?"

"I don't know, man."

"Even if we run it for just a few months, now, while business is booming, we could do at least twenty or thirty apiece. I have a connection in LA who can probably unload every ounce we get. He caters for the A-list crowd. We could get top dollar. And you could finally pay back what you've been owing me for years."

Ryan slowly backed away from the door and returned to her room. She tried to tell herself she hadn't heard correctly. Dennis and Adam were friends in high school. Simply being connected to a powerful family like that opened wide the door of possibilities. Her brother wouldn't be stupid enough to steal from Adam and get that door slammed in his face, and possibly another one clanked shut, one with bars and concrete and neighbors called inmates. Ryan slipped back into bed and pulled the covers over her head, not wanting to believe what she'd heard. Tomorrow would be soon enough to question her brother and learn the last ten minutes had been a dream.

The next morning, Ryan woke up early. She wanted to speak with Dennis while their parents were still sleeping. She didn't want an argument. But she wanted and would get the answers to explain what she heard last night. She knocked lightly, then checked the knob. The door was unlocked.

"Denny," she whispered, approaching his bed. She gently shook his shoulder. "Hey, wake up. It's important."

"What the heck time is it?" Dennis asked, his eyes squinting in Ryan's direction. "What's going on? Is it Dad?"

"No, Dad's fine." Ryan sat on the bed. "I want to ask you about something that I heard but I don't want to argue, okay?"

"If you think the question might start an argument, then maybe you'd better not ask it."

"I have to, but I don't want us to start yelling again and wake up Dad."

Dennis was wide-awake now. His eyes were hard as he glared at her. "What, you heard me talking to Luke about a new enterprise?"

Ryan hadn't expected Dennis to admit they'd had a conversation. Maybe what she thought she heard was a big misunderstanding.

"Yes, and it sounded as though you were going to swap out the more expensive meat that Adam raises for a lesser quality and make a huge profit."

"And?"

"Are you kidding me?" Ryan screeched, forgetting about the need to keep her voice low. "You've got a great thing going at Breedlove Beef. Why ruin a great job with someone like Adam to make a quick, illegal buck with Luke?"

"Exactly." Dennis laughed as his head flopped back on the pillow. "You know Luke is always scheming. We were running the numbers, talking what-ifs. I think Adam could have paid me more. He's definitely got the money. But I like working at the estate. Plus, I'm not going to steal from my sister's boyfriend. So stop worrying, girl. Luke's just talking. And I'm just humoring him by going along."

It was a civil exchange, pleasant even. Ryan made herself comfortable on the bed, chatting with Dennis for almost an hour. She admitted how much she liked Adam, but denied being ready to become his missus as Dennis suggested. They talked about being back in Las Vegas, both admitting it being better the second time around. But mostly they talked about Joe, and finding a kidney. Ryan enjoyed spending the evening with her brother and hoped the camaraderie would continue. Returning to Vegas she thought about Adam, the sexual attraction and deepening feelings, and admitted that however uncomfortable and inconvenient, she hoped their spending time together would continue, too.

Fifteen

The year was winding down and, after today, so too would Adam's workload. The first shipments of Wagyu had been delivered. Business owners were thrilled, customers were satisfied, positive product reviews continued, and orders were brisk. That's why he was still in the office well after the sun had gone down, and after putting in almost a full day at CANN International. His body felt every hour he'd worked, and every long day for the past two months. That's why with operations running smoothly, he was taking a week off. The barn would see him next year.

Even being tired, Adam bypassed his truck parked in the lot and began walking the short distance to his house. After being cooped up in offices for most of the day, the cool night air was refreshing and there wasn't anything quite so beautiful as a midnight-blue Nevada sky.

Tapping his Bluetooth earphone, he pulled out his phone and called Ryan.

"Hey, baby."

"Hey."

"How is the woman with the healing hands?"

"Would you stop with that?" she asked him.

But he heard the smile in her voice. "I'm only saying what's true. And check this out. I'm booking my appointment soon and when I do, I get a discount."

"You will?"

"Absolutely. I told Mom and my assistant, Olivia, about Integrative Healing. If they haven't already, both will be calling soon. They've also promised to spread the word."

"Wow, Adam, thank you! The best marketing for services is word of mouth, so I really appreciate you telling others about the business. You'll absolutely get a discount."

"Any news on your dad, and finding a donor?"

"Not yet, but it might be me. My blood type and Dad's is the same."

While a fairly common procedure with relatively low risks, removing a kidney was still major surgery. Ryan would be left with only one. What if somehow it was damaged? Would she then be in search of a donor? Knowing how Ryan felt about her father, Adam didn't voice his concerns. If Nicholas needed anything donated, the brothers would be in line to help him get well.

"Two more tests are needed to see if I'm a true candidate."

"You almost sound excited."

"I'm hopeful. So far, no one else has been a match. His name has already been placed on the donor list, but the wait through that avenue can be anywhere from six months to a year. I'm not sure Dad… We want him to get the transplant as soon as possible."

Adam heard what sounded like the beep of doors unlocked with a car fob. "Where are you?"

"Just leaving the office."

"This late?" Said even while remembering he'd just left, too.

"Yeah. I had a walk-in right as we were about to close up, then did some paperwork. Plus I'm still catching up from all the time spent helping to take care of Dad."

"Are you headed home?"

"Yes."

"Want some company?"

A slight pause and then, "Sure."

"I'm on my way." Adam spun on his boot and headed back to his pickup. He was suddenly not tired at all.

Just outside of Breedlove's city limits, his phone rang.

"Hey, Miguel, what's up?"

"Hey, boss. I'm not sure. Are you in town where you can come by real quick?"

"I'm just outside of town on my way to Vegas. What's going on?"

"I just opened a package of beef marked Wagyu instead of Black Angus. I'm not an expert on the new beef, but it didn't look like either of the stock we raise. Didn't cook up like it, either."

Adam let out a long, slow breath. How could this mix-up happen, especially since the restaurant wasn't serving Wagyu? Minutes into the weeklong vacation he'd planned, it was the last thing he wanted to hear. But quality was where Breedlove Beef hung its hat. There was no way he could leave errors to chance. So he checked the mirrors, made a U-turn and headed to BBs.

He pulled into the parking lot a short time later. Since it was the holidays and many were out of town, the restaurant wasn't as crowded as usual. He pulled out a key and entered through the side door, then headed straight to the kitchen, where he found Miguel sweating over a grill full of meat.

"Hey, boss."

"Miguel." Adam stepped closer to the grill, examining its contents. "Where's the meat you called about?"

"Hang on a sec. I put it up so it wouldn't get mixed up with these orders."

Adam watched as Miguel worked the grill like a maestro, delivering to-order doneness from rare to well in choices from burgers to steaks. To be admired, even in Adam's state of chagrin. After finishing the orders, Miguel pulled the towel from around his neck and wiped his face. He turned to the other stainless steel counter and uncovered a patty on a saucer.

"This is the burger from the package," he said, handing it to Adam, before continuing to the fridge.

Adam eyed the burger, smelled it, then broke off a piece to taste.

Miguel walked back to where Adam stood. "This is the package."

It wasn't discernible to Adam's eye, but one whiff and his suspicions were as heightened as Miguel's were, and one bite was all he needed to drop the saucer back onto the counter. That wasn't Breedlove anything, Wagyu or otherwise. He opened the packet to inspect the raw meat, then the packaging itself, which was definitely from his facility.

"Do me a favor. Put this back in the fridge, but when you leave tonight, take it with you, okay? I don't want any chance for that to be served, but we need to keep it so I can find out its origins and how it ended up with our label."

"Because it isn't Black Angus, either, huh?"

Adam shook his head.

"I wonder what it is?"

Adam placed the Stetson he'd removed when entering back on his head. "I don't know, but I'm going to find out. On second thought, hand me that package. I've got to figure out where this meat came from and how it was mislabeled. Have the wrong customer get a lower-quality product than was ordered, one who takes their complaint to the media, and our reputation could be damaged. It's too early in the game for us to take that chance."

Back in his truck, Adam called Ryan. "Sorry, baby, change in plans."

"Is everything okay?"

"Probably, but I got a call regarding something at the plant and need to head back there. I probably should have Dennis meet me there, too. Call you later?"

"Sure."

"Rain check on keeping you company?"

"Anytime."

Adam's call to Dennis went to voice mail. He made a couple others. By the time Adam reached the plant, Stan and Will were waiting for him. They followed Adam into a break room.

"What's going on, boss?" Stan asked.

"Whatever it was sounded important," Will said.

Adam pulled out the package of meat from Miguel. "Take a look at this, guys, and tell me what you think."

Will gave Adam a look. "You pulled me away from a warm fireplace to look at ground round?"

Adam watched as Will pulled off a chunk of the

meat and brought it up to his nose. He made a face and examined it closer.

"Where did you get this?" he asked.

"It was in a package boasting a Wagyu label delivered to the restaurant this morning."

"This sure as hell isn't Wagyu," Stan said.

"It isn't Black Angus, either," Will replied. "Not our stock, anyway."

"The package has our label," Adam said. "It had to have come from this plant."

"Where's Dennis?" Stan asked.

"I called but he didn't answer, left a message about a fire that needed to be quickly put out."

The sound of the outer door opening cut off further conversation. All three men looked toward the door.

Dennis hurried into the room rubbing his hands together for warmth. His hair was tousled and his eyes were bloodshot. Adam figured he'd been drinking, or keeping company with a woman, or both.

"I just got your message, Adam. What's going on?"

"A mystery," Adam said, nodding for Stan to give the cellophane-wrapped meat he held to Dennis. "We need to understand how that meat got in packaging labeled Wagyu."

"Likely human error," Dennis said.

He took the package from Stan, examined the contents and placed the meat to his nose. "Perhaps the package got mislabeled."

Will slowly shook his head. "I don't know where that meat came from, but it's not from our breeds."

"That's impossible," Dennis said, looking between the three men. "Unless a stray cow wandered into the herd somehow. Don't worry, Adam. I'll get to the bottom of it."

"Stan, Will, I need you to work with Dennis. I'll be here first thing tomorrow, too. We have to make sure this is a onetime error. It cannot happen again."

Sixteen

Ryan's hands slowly glided just above the woman lying facedown on her table. Her eyes were closed as she worked, fingers hovering over the areas where she felt energy blocked, or strains of the body lacking ease, being ill at ease, dis-eased. She completed the procedure and after a moment, gently placed her hand on the client's back.

"We're finished," she said softly.

"Are you sure?"

Ryan chuckled. Her work often relaxed clients to the point of falling asleep. The peaceful, healing atmosphere was an addictive one that people often didn't want to leave.

Ryan chuckled. "Yes, Miss Olivia, I'm quite sure. Would you like me to help you? Here." Ryan stepped forward as the older woman turned and used her arms to raise off the table. "That's it, go slowly. All of that energy is still settling. Some get light-headed if they move too quickly."

Miss Olivia sat up, turned her head one way and then the other.

"How do you feel?"

"Why, it's the most interesting thing. It feels as though I just had a massage but you barely touched me at all!"

Ryan reiterated what she'd told Miss Olivia before starting the process, how blocked, nervous and other negative energies affected the body and how the practice of Reiki helped bring the flow back into balance. "I felt quite a bit of tension around your neck and shoulders," she finished. "That's where you seem to hold a lot of stress. So try to relax, okay?"

"That's easier said than done these days. We're so busy at the office that I finally told Adam, look, I'm an old lady. I can't do all of this by myself."

She eased down from the table and walked over to where her shoes rested in front of a chair.

"So we're going to hire somebody and I told him the sooner the better."

"I'm glad to hear that, Miss Olivia. It sounds like everyone is a bit surprised at how successful everything turned out."

"Oh, not me. I've known Adam for many years and one thing I can tell you. When he makes up his mind about something, know that it will get done and better than anyone else could do it. He's a driven man, but a good one." She lowered her voice as her cornflower blue eyes twinkled. "And he's single. But you know that."

"Yes, I do." Ryan looked at her watch. While Olivia put on her shoes, Ryan retrieved her personal items from off the credenza. "Just as Adam referred you, if you tell someone and they come in for an appointment, you'll receive 20 percent off on your next visit."

"Whether or not I get the discount, sign me up."

Ryan walked Olivia to the door and gave her a hug. For a woman who'd turned seventy last year, she was in great health, stress and all. It had been a pleasure to treat her. With another appointment scheduled for a half hour later, she rushed back to ready the room. As she reached her office, the phone rang. She rushed in to grab it, tapped the speaker button and sat down at her desk.

"Integrative Healing, Ryan speaking."

"Hello, Ryan, it's Victoria Breedlove."

Ryan stopped, surprised at the call. She quickly recovered. "Hi, Victoria."

"I know it's the middle of a workday. Is this a good time?"

"My next client is in a half hour. Your timing is interesting as I just finished up with Adam's assistant, Miss Olivia."

"She told me that she was going to come see you. Adam was very impressed with all you've shared with him about your business, and recommended you to several of us."

In the moment Adam sounded like such a great guy and considering her brother's conversation that she'd overheard, Ryan felt like a jerk.

"Are you calling to make an appointment?"

"No, and I'd love to go into detail when you have more time but I'm calling with an invitation. You might recall the Thanksgiving conversation I had with your mom discussing the CANN Foundation and the various events held to raise funding for any number of charitable causes."

"Yes, I remember."

"In February, we're hosting an event called Loving You. Contributors have paid handsomely for a two-hour pampering at the hotel, followed by a private lunch. Would you be open to have one of your services included as part of that package, perhaps the energetic work that you've done on Adam and now Olivia? You'd be compensated, of course," she hurriedly added. "And have the opportunity to market your services to high-end clientele, and they'd have an opportunity to learn about different ways to feel better. It could be a win-win for both of us."

"Wow, Victoria, this was totally unexpected and a wonderful opportunity."

"I was hoping you'd think so, and would like to set up a meeting for later this week. Is there a time that works for you, for either lunch or dinner?"

"Dinner would definitely be preferable. But can we meet next week instead?"

"Sure, sweetheart, either Monday or Tuesday if possible. I'll look forward to hearing from you."

Ryan ended the call and looked at the clock on her desk. She had a little free time before her next appointment. She headed down the hall and passed Brooklyn's office. The door opened suddenly. Both women jumped. "Oh! Crap, you scared me," Brooklyn said.

"Me, too."

They continued into the break area.

"How's your morning?" Brooklyn asked.

"Okay. I have a nutrition consultation in about twenty minutes. What about you?"

"Nothing for about an hour. I'm thankful for the break." Brooklyn pulled a powdered product from the cabinet. "Want a protein smoothie?"

Ryan shook her head.

"You probably need one."

"Okay, Mom."

Brooklyn smiled. Ryan managed one, too. Her business partner's mother-henning was legendary.

Brooklyn whipped up the drinks, poured a glass and handed one to Ryan. "This is delicious," Ryan said after a drink of the creamy concoction. "And you're right. I did need it. Thank you."

The doorbell buzzed. The women looked at each other.

"Walk-in?" Brooklyn queried.

Ryan headed for the door. "We'll soon see."

She reached the foyer and looked at the security camera video screen placed discreetly behind a large potted plant. The pensive-looking face on the other side of the door was the last one that she expected. She hurried to open it.

"Adam?"

Upon seeing her, Adam's face broke into a smile. "I need a massage, badly," he said, giving her a hug. "Can you fit me in?"

"My next appointment is in about fifteen minutes but sure, we'll work something out. Come on back."

Ryan saw that Brooklyn's office was empty and continued down the hall to the break room. "Before we get started, I'd like you to meet my partner."

They entered the break room. Brooklyn had taken a seat at the table and was thumbing through a magazine. Seeing Adam, she jumped up.

"Hi!"

Ryan chuckled. "Obviously you already know, this is Adam. Adam, meet my business partner and best friend, Brooklyn Chase."

"It's a pleasure to meet you, Adam," Brooklyn gushed. "You're even more handsome in person."

"You've been researched," Ryan explained.

"Thoroughly," Brooklyn added, completely unapologetic. "Spending time with my bestie, you had to be checked out."

"I guess you found all in order since I'm not getting kicked out."

"So far, so good," Brooklyn said.

While Brooklyn chatted with Adam, Ryan went for her phone. She texted her nutrition client and was able to push that appointment to later that day. She returned to the break room, where Adam waited, alone. They hugged. Ryan learned her man hadn't been joking about needing a massage. His strong back and broad shoulders felt as tight as a drum.

"All right, guy," Ryan said, after checking to make sure the massage room was ready. "We now have a full forty minutes. Let's get started."

She handled Adam as she would any client, giving him a moment of privacy to undress before reentering the room. There were none of Adam's usual flirtations and innuendos. He was quiet and remained so as she began her work.

After doing a quick energy scan, she started on his shoulders. "What happened?" she asked, her voice as soothing as the light New Age music wafting from hidden speakers. "You are as tense as I've ever felt you. What has you so stressed?"

"I was up most of the night dealing with a problem at the plant," he explained after a pause. "We believe it's handled but can't be totally sure. Because we weren't able to determine how the problem occurred, we can't guarantee it won't be repeated."

"What was the problem?"

Adam began explaining what had happened after talking with her, the call he'd gotten from Miguel and what was discovered.

"Dennis believes a stray cow from another farm somehow ended up in our pasture. There are other cows in the area but there are miles between properties. It's a far-fetched explanation at best, but the only one we had."

With every sentence Ryan heard, her heart sank further and further into despair. She believed she immediately knew how the foreign product got into Adam's plant. She had to remove her hands from his skin, they began to shake so badly. "I need to get a special oil from the storeroom," she whispered. "Be right back."

Ryan ran to her office, closed the door and took several deep, calming breaths to prevent what felt like an oncoming panic attack. She felt nauseous. Dennis had sworn that she'd misinterpreted what she heard. She so wanted to believe that was true, but could what Adam have told her be coincidence? Was there really another explanation to how foreign beef ended up in his plant's freezer? Every option to remedy her dilemma led to a headache. She felt one coming on right now and headed toward the herbs in the break room cabinet.

She reentered the massage room as quietly as possible. Adam looked up. "Where's the oil?"

"Oh, we were out. It's okay." Ryan walked over to a tray filled with various tubes and bottles. "I have something else that will work just as well."

"Are you all right?" he asked, his eyes narrowing as he continued to observe her.

"Lie down and relax, Mr. Breedlove. Don't worry

about me. It's my job to make sure you feel better, and that's exactly what I'm going to do."

She concentrated and placed all of her focus into what she was doing. She felt the knots began to loosen as Adam finally relaxed. When she finished, he was almost sleeping. He turned over and pulled her to him.

"There's one more muscle you need to massage," he murmured, guiding her hand toward his groin.

She playfully pulled her hand away. "Later, I promise," she said. "Right now I need to prepare for my next client. How do you feel?"

"Like I've been touched by an angel," he said, sliding off the table and reaching for his clothes. "And totally cured."

Back-to-back clients kept Ryan busy for the next two hours but she found enough time to send Dennis a text, short and to the point.

You. Lied.

She didn't receive a reply from him. She wasn't expecting any.

"So here's a scenario," Ryan began after walking into Brooklyn's office and plopping down in a visitor chair. "It involves three friends. Friend number one overhears friend number two plotting something against friend number three. Friend number one loves both of them in different ways and knows that if she tells friend number three what she heard number two say about them, it could be very problematic. Should friend number one say anything?"

"Let me think about that." Brooklyn picked up a beautiful amethyst crystal and rolled it around in her hand. After a few seconds, she set it down and walked around her desk to where Ryan sat.

"I think you, I mean friend number one, should follow this." Brooklyn placed a hand over Ryan's heart. "It will never steer her wrong."

Later that afternoon, as Ryan worked with her nutrition client toward a natural solution that would reduce her high blood pressure, eliminate type 2 diabetes and balance her cholesterol, a possible next step for Ryan's situation began to form. After finishing the consultation and walking her client to the door, she returned to her office and opened her tablet. She clicked on a search engine. Ryan's hands hovered over the tablet keys as she thought of the right way to phrase the search. After beginning and deleting several possibilities, she typed *listening devices* and clicked Enter, and a whole new world appeared on her screen.

Thirty minutes later she'd ordered a product that she didn't know existed thirty-one minutes ago. There were mixed emotions about using it, teetering on all kinds of ethical and moral fine lines. Soon, she'd be able to listen in on Dennis's conversations and read his texts. If Breedlove Beef was mentioned, she wasn't sure how she'd handle it. But at least she'd know the truth.

Seventeen

An old year went out. A new year came in. But the problem with the mystery meat did not go away. It became worse, which caused Adam to take drastic action. He wearily looked up as someone tapped on his office door. "Everyone rounded up?"

Olivia nodded. "They're ready, boss."

"Okay." Adam rose from his chair and reached for the suit jacket hanging on a hook. Most days he came to the plant dressed in flannel and denim. Today wasn't like the others. In fact, life at Breedlove Beef Processing Center hadn't been the same since he'd gotten the call from Miguel. There'd been more calls regarding inferior product, and meetings with Dennis, Rusty and the supervisors over each detail. A plan had been devised and was ready to be implemented. He slid on a finely spun wool suit jacket, ran a hand through his curls and headed to where the employees had gathered for this mandatory meeting. Many didn't know why it had been called, but one look at their boss's dress and demeanor, and chatter rapidly diminished before disappearing altogether. By the time Adam reached the front of the room you could hear a fly land on a cow's tail.

"We have a problem," he began, as his gaze slowly took in every face in the room. "Somehow meat from cows not raised at Breedlove ranch has found its way into this plant. It didn't walk in, didn't amble into the building on four hooves. So that can only mean that someone working here is mishandling product.

"Recently, a very astute chef called me, gravely concerned about a packet of meat that was supposed to be Wagyu but was in fact a type of beef not bred on this ranch. Since then we've received several more calls from the high-end restaurants clamoring for our product, but we also received a couple of calls from Black Angus customers who said the meat wasn't the same. I believe whoever is behind this switching up of product felt it was okay to throw in a few pounds of average meat and sell the Wagyu for a nice little profit. I believe that person most likely can hear me right now."

Adam took in the various reactions. His eyes narrowed as he observed those he felt might be culprits. He'd gotten Dennis's and Rusty's input on who they thought might be behind the problem, and he had a couple ideas of his own. But no one would be called into question right now. Adam would strike, but only when the time was right.

"I'm implementing a few changes effective Monday, three days from now. Each employee will be issued a badge that will be required for entry. The floor is being reconfigured, with the Wagyu operation completely separate from the Black Angus in a room that will be locked at all times.

"No one is being looked at to be fired, yet. But some of you will be questioned and all of you will be monitored. If you're guilty and come forth voluntarily, come to my office and talk face-to-face, there may be a chance that any criminal charges that we're considering might be taken off the table. Sometimes there are extenuating circumstances, a right reason for something done wrong. If you come to me, admit what you did and tell me why, and agree to the terms I'll require regarding your termination, you'll still be fired. But you might remain free."

The meeting ended with the employees somberly filing out of the office. Finally only Adam and Dennis remained.

"This is all my fault," Dennis said with a heavy sigh.

"More than forty people help to run this operation. If one person is at fault, it's me."

"I manage the operation. It happened on my watch!"

"Have you ever seen a situation anywhere similar to this?"

"No, but I haven't worked at a plant with this quality of meat, either." He placed a hand on Adam's shoulder. "I had your back in high school. I've got it now. We'll get to the bottom of this, bro. Hang in there."

Adam nodded and walked out of the room with Dennis, heading to his car and a meeting at CANN. But his mind stayed on Breedlove Beef Processing, and the person trying to ruin what he'd built.

Eighteen

As had become her practice, Ryan walked her latest client to the door and gave her a hug. This time she continued outside.

"Are you leaving?" the client asked.

Ryan shook her head. "Just getting a breath of fresh air."

"I don't know how fresh it is, but…see you next time!"

"Okay," Ryan said, while laughing. "Have a beautiful rest of your day."

Ryan watched the tall, gorgeous redhead walk to her car. She closed her eyes, stretched and performed exercises that allowed her to release the energy absorbed when working on others, especially important when the client was troubled and shared with her aspects of their dark lives. Practitioners such as Ryan often became pseudo-counselors and therapists as well. Ryan hoped she'd gain the courage to leave a man who was verbally abusive and make room for one who deserved her.

That wasn't the only conversation that required another deep breath, but that would come later. Ryan walked back inside. Her next appointment was for a massage, a new client named Fred. He'd booked through the phone app so his first name was all she knew about him. That was fine, because once he was on the table his body would tell her everything else she needed to know.

Ryan stopped by the restroom, then entered her room and began preparing it for the appointment. She changed the music from the Asian-influenced sounds currently playing to a list with more classical tones. She switched out the sheets, sprayed them with lavender and had just picked up oil for the diffuser when the door buzzed. She walked over and pushed the intercom button.

"Fred?"

"Yes," he mumbled.

"When you hear the buzzer, turn the knob and have a seat in the foyer. I'll be right out."

Ryan lit the diffuser, raised the dim lights a notch and went to greet her client. She opened the door and turned toward the chairs. They were empty.

Where is he?

She turned to the other side of the room. "Adam?"

"Um," he said in that same muffled voice. "Call me Fred."

"Oh my God, are you…" She burst out laughing and ran into his arms. They kissed, softly at first and then another, longer exchange.

Ryan ended it and led the way down the hall. "You nut!" she said after they'd entered the room and she'd closed the door. "I can't believe you're back so soon. And what's with this Fred act?"

Adam shrugged. "The unexpected makes life more fun."

"Sometimes…"

"Right. Sometimes."

Ryan chuckled again. "So, Fred, I will leave the room as you get undressed, and comfortable on the table, and return in two minutes."

Adam began unbuttoning his shirt. "I wouldn't think of it. In fact, why don't you take off your clothes, too. We can massage each other."

"That sounds incredibly tempting. You surprising me like this is a definite turn-on. But these walls are thin and the rooms are full. Suyin is performing acupuncture next door. Hearing grunts and moans from the other room could have her poking needles in the wrong place."

Having sat to remove his shoes and socks, Adam stood to take off his pants and boxers. "Fine," he said, strolling over in all of his naked glory and pulling Ryan into an embrace. "I wouldn't want anyone getting poked in the wrong place. But will you let me poke something later?"

Ryan hugged him, choking back a laugh as her hands skimmed his bare skin. "I can't with you," she whispered. "Get that fine ass up on my table."

He smiled, got on the table and tried to pull her on with him. She jerked her arm away. "Will you behave?" she asked through clenched teeth. "Now, over on your stomach, please."

He huffed, and Ryan caught a childlike expression that had probably gotten him out of trouble more than once. "You're no fun."

"Perhaps, but you'll feel better."

"Does that mean this appointment has a happy ending?" Ryan smacked his butt, then kissed it, before covering the firm gift of nature with a thin sheet and beginning her work.

For several minutes she worked in silence, starting with his feet and moving methodically upward. She was a naturopathic doctor who worked on bodies for a living. Being dispassionate should come naturally but with this particular client, being a woman came first, followed closely by being a lover of fine male specimens. Still, she worked with quiet efficiency, paying attention to physical knots and energetic blocks and clearing both before moving on. When she reached his thigh and massaged out a particularly tight muscle, he groaned aloud.

"Having fun yet?" she asked.

"Best time of my life."

She chuckled. "Which business is all of this stress, tension and nervousness from, the ranch or the hotel?"

"Yes." They both laughed. "Remember me telling you about that weird incident when Miguel received a package of beef with our label that was not from my ranch?"

Ryan's hand slowed, but for only a second. "Yes."

"I was hoping it was a onetime fluke. It wasn't."

"He got another package of the same meat?"

"Not Miguel. Another customer received it. This time it wasn't the ground Wagyu but a steak."

"How is that happening? I don't understand."

"Someone is stealing the prime Wagyu and replacing it with cheap stock. As to how it's happening, I don't understand that, either. Not yet. But we're working on it."

"We?"

"Me and management. Your brother, Dennis, and Rusty, the assistant manager. Changes were made that are going to make it very difficult for more thefts to occur. If the culprits get past all of the security we've set up, then I'll personally give them the same amount that they stole."

Later that day, Ryan called Dennis on his office line. He hadn't answered calls from her cell phone but now he picked up.

"Breedlove Beef, Dennis Washington."

"Is it Breedlove Beef?" Ryan asked, her voice deadly calm. "Or is it the beef you and Luke somehow switched out to make big bucks on the black market?"

"You don't know what you're talking about. Look, I'm busy and can't talk right now."

"What was the figure I overheard that night? A couple hundred thou—"

Dennis hung up on her. Ryan was livid. She was barely able to make it through the rest of the day. After her last appointment she got into her car and pulled out of the parking lot with one destination in mind, the Breedlove estate. She needed to have a conversation with Dennis, have him prove that he was not behind what was happening at the plant. She couldn't know what was going on and stay quiet. It just wasn't right.

Ryan reached the gates to the Breedlove property with no clear plan. She didn't want Adam to know she was there, but knew the guard might call and announce her arrival. Fortunately, the guard had been there on one of her previous visits. He opened the gate and waved her through. What she hoped was her biggest hurdle had just been jumped. Now all she had to do was get through to her brother. Ryan pulled into the plant parking lot. She kept an eye out for either Adam's sports car or truck as she hurried up the walk and reached for the door. If she saw Adam, she'd tell him the truth. That she was there to speak with her brother. Hopefully he wouldn't ask what about.

It wasn't until finding out the door was locked that Ryan noticed the bell on the door frame. She rang it. A young man came to the door.

"Yes, may I help you?"

Ryan poured on the charm. "Hi, I'm Ryan, Dennis's sister. I need to speak to him."

The man hesitated before opening the door wider. "Sure, come in." He led her to where a security guard leaned against a stand. "This lady says she's here to see Dennis."

Ryan introduced herself, then remembered her client, Olivia. "If you'll let her know I'm here she can help me if he's preoccupied."

Mentioning Olivia did the trick. Her client was surprised to see her but brought her up to the offices on the second floor. When told Ryan was there to see her, Dennis said he was busy. That if she wanted to speak to him, she'd be waiting awhile.

She waited. By the time Dennis finally opened his door, Olivia and most of the other workers had gone home. A good thing, since Ryan's patience had ticked away with the time. She saw Dennis and lit into him.

"You've made me wait an hour, so I'll tell you what. You've got five minutes to convince me that you're not guilty."

"You've got five seconds to get out of here before I call security."

"Fine, call security. They'd be very interested to hear what I overheard, the scheme to make big money on high-priced beef."

"You're crazy, kid. Making stuff up."

"I can't keep quiet, Dennis," Ryan said, working to calm down. She tried another tactic, hoping to find an ounce of compassion in her brother's cold heart. "Adam and I are dating. I'm falling for him. Things might get serious. How can I know what's going on and not say anything about it?"

"Because I know things I haven't shared with him about you," Dennis said. "You're standing there in your moral dress, as if your life is perfect. Have you told Adam your secrets, little sister? About how you're adopted? And how your birth mother ended up in jail after committing fraud to get drugs?"

He went on about how lucky she was to have been raised in a "normal" household, and how different it could have been.

"I'm not ashamed of my past and in time will tell Adam everything, including what I know about—"

"What?" Dennis interrupted. "What exactly do you think you know? I'd really like to hear it."

"So would I."

Ryan whirled around to see Adam standing in the doorway. Dennis had obviously seen him first. That's why she was interrupted.

"Is there something either of you need to tell me?" he asked.

"It's a sibling squabble, Adam," Dennis said. "Nothing to do with you."

"The fight sounded pretty serious. I heard the yelling from downstairs." He looked at Ryan. "Are you okay?"

Ryan fought to hold it together. "I will be," she answered. "Sorry to bring this kind of drama to your business."

She pushed past him, ran out the door and wondered what all Adam had heard.

Nineteen

A week had passed since the confrontation, since he'd gone back to the office and found Dennis and Ryan locked in a heated argument, had overheard talk about family and keeping secrets. Dennis had sworn it was about Ryan. Later, Ryan said it involved Luke. But she wouldn't say anything else, and that bothered him. What had Luke done to her and why wouldn't she share it? At the mere thought that he could have hurt her, Adam's hands balled into fists. That following Monday Adam had met with Dennis outside the office, had first invited him to go riding (Dennis didn't do horses), then to a round of golf (he didn't do clubs, not iron ones, anyway), then finally settled on drinks on the bar side of BBs restaurant. When asked the reason for them getting together, Adam had been purposely vague.

"There's been a lot going on," he'd casually replied. "Between CANN and the ranch I've spent too much time in offices. Plus, you and I haven't had a chance to just hang out since work started. Thought it would be good to kick back for a minute, off the clock."

Of course, there'd been more to it. The more relaxed the environment and in turn, Dennis, the better the chances he'd slip up and say something Adam needed to know. Unlike Rusty, he didn't think his old high school friend was the one stealing the Wagyu. But he believed Dennis knew more than he'd shared. Adam couldn't figure out what that was, which was why in addition to hiring a private investigator, he'd called an impromptu meeting with his brothers to beat their brains about it.

"I think he's lying," Nick said, after Adam had caught them up with what had happened since last Friday. He cracked another peanut, tossed the shells on the concrete, before throwing up the nut and catching it in his mouth.

The brothers were out on Adam's massive patio, their chairs haphazardly placed around the roaring firepit. Shells littered the floor around Nick and Christian, a stainless steel bowl filled with peanuts on a table between them. Bottles of beer were scattered about. Adam carefully snipped a cigar.

Noah stood and leaned against a thick wooden beam anchoring the pergola. "I do, too. I think he's in on it."

"So does Rusty," Adam replied. "He spent the weekend and a lot of hours this week glued to a split screen running back surveillance video, hours and hours of tape from cameras mounted inside and outside. He was looking for Dennis specifically."

"What did he find?" Christian asked.

"Nothing." Adam reached for a lighter on the table in front of him and began toasting the cigar from a box he'd recently received as a Christmas gift.

"It's frustrating because until the renovation last weekend our focus regarding theft was for the actual cows. Heck, when it comes to the pastures, especially West Wagyu, there are probably more cameras than birds."

The brothers laughed.

"I remember you telling me about the company's humor at your request," Christian said. "What was the line you said the owner kept saying?"

Adam placed the cigar in an ashtray and stroked his chin. "Oh, man, don't make me hear it again."

"He said Adam was after bird-gulars."

Nick burst out laughing. In stark contrast, Noah slowly shook his head. "That was so bad."

Adam finally gave in and smiled. At the time, it had been funny. Not now.

"We put cameras by the doors to catch anyone walking out with large boxes or packages. If anyone were to steal, which I honestly doubted would happen, we thought it would be a steak or two here, or maybe a slab of ribs there. We didn't have cameras in the cooling room, or in the chop area right outside. So far, no one I've questioned has raised a red flag. They are good, honest, hardworking employees. That's what their résumés and references showed. That's why I hired them."

"Obviously there's a bad apple," Christian said.

"Obviously," Adam agreed. He pulled on the cigar, the circles he blew dissipating in the night air. "But we'll find him and we'll cut him out…before he spoils the whole bunch."

One by one the brothers dispersed and headed home. Adam walked into the house and turned on his big-screen TV, looking for sports. He found a tennis match but was too restless to watch it. He decided to head over to BBs, and had just reached for his jacket when the phone rang.

"Ryan."

"Hey, Adam."

"Babe, what's going on? I'm giving you the space it seems you need but we've got to talk, and soon."

"You're right, Adam. We do need to talk. I'm sorry for how I've been acting lately, about the argument at your office and that I've been pretty much silent since then. There is a lot that I need to share with you, especially now."

Adam perched on a barstool. "What's going on now?"

"All of the tests have come back. I'm a perfect match. Six weeks from now, I'm going to give my dad a kidney."

"You were hoping to help him. I'm so glad things turned out as you wanted."

"Me, too. And with the surgery scheduled, I don't want any secrets between us."

"Are you at home, Ryan? I can come over now."

"Not tonight. I'm working on a time-sensitive project. But soon, okay?"

"Okay."

"Adam?"

"Yes."

"I…I'll see you soon."

Adam ended the call, placing the phone in his pocket as he reached for his jacket and headed to his truck. He was glad that Ryan called him, but what she'd shared had him very concerned. The research he'd done on kidney transplants and donors had left him feeling better about that operation. But what else did Ryan have to tell him? What were the secrets that she needed to share?

Did they involve Luke or Dennis? Were his brothers right that Dennis was lying? Was one of Ryan's secrets that she was lying, too?

Twenty

Ryan sat cross-legged in her bed, staring at her cell phone. She'd already picked it up and placed it back down several times. Somehow she felt these moments, right now, were the last of the world as she knew it. Once she opened the application, accessed the information and printed it out, her life would not be the same. She couldn't say all of the different ways that it might change, but it could not return to the way it was now.

She reached for the small instruction booklet that had come with the cell tracking and listening device. There was really no need for her to read it again. It was straightforward, easy. She'd been shocked and appalled at how the tracker worked, what all it could do, how easy it had been to install and how for over a week she'd had complete access to her brother's cell phone without him having a clue. For all that time she refused to dial the number, would ignore the buzz on her phone indi-

cating that her brother was either making or receiving
a call. After last Friday night's blowup had been the
first time. She'd just arrived home and was sitting in
her car, trying to process what had happened and forget
the look of confusion on Adam's face, the questions in
his eyes. That's when the phone had buzzed and she'd
picked it up and tapped the key to listen in. Within seconds, Dennis's voice came through so loud and clear
Ryan had held her breath, certain he could hear her,
half thinking he could see her, too. Pangs of guilt as-
sailed her for being a lurker but once she heard what
was being discussed, she couldn't hang up.

*"...I'm telling you, Luke, this is serious! I don't know
how much of our conversation he heard."*

"And I'm telling you that you need to chill out."

Ryan's jaw dropped. Luke was in on it. Then again,
she should have known.

*"There's no chilling out. Pandora is out of the box
with cameras rolling!"*

Ryan could feel the panic in her brother's voice.

*"But he doesn't suspect you, man, he trusts you.
Didn't you tell me that you were the only one with the
key to the good stuff?"*

Ryan eased out of her car and gently closed the door.
The instructions had assured her that there was no way
she was being detected, that her spying was not notice-
able in any way and could not be traced. Didn't matter.
Only sheer force of will kept her from tiptoeing once
she'd opened the door.

"No, man," her brother was saying when she'd refocused on the call from that night. *"You're not hearing me. This stuff is over. The gig is up. That plant is
locked down worse than prison. They're gunning for*

who jacked up those orders, who switched that meat, and I'm square in their crosshairs. Getting away with this will take a miracle."

"You owe me too much money to try calling shots. This was the way you came up with to pay me back, so you need to keep making it happen."

"There's no way, man, too risky."

"What about Ryan?"

Ryan gasped and quickly slapped her hand over her mouth.

"What about Ryan?" Dennis repeated back to Luke.

Ryan listened intently. Yeah, what about her?

"Didn't you say they were dating?" Luke asked.

"Yes, and?"

"Bring her into it. She already knows and according to you won't say anything about it."

"No, she's won't say anything. She's got secrets, too."

"Then she'd be the perfect middleman to drive the product off the property. Since they're dating, seeing her car would be normal. It's actually perfect, man. I can't believe you didn't think of it."

Ryan waited, her heart beating out of her chest.

"Ryan would never agree to do it. And I can't force her."

Her relief had been palpable. It felt good to know that her brother wouldn't sell her all the way out. What he said made her decision more painful. But it didn't change her mind. She'd checked her brother's texts and as she figured, incriminating conversations had occurred between her brother and Luke, proof of exactly what they'd been doing and possibly even information on where some of the beef had been sold. She'd give Dennis one more chance to tell Adam himself. If he didn't, she would. So after taking a deep breath she sent

Dennis a text, relayed that information and attached a screenshot of one of his damning texts to prove she wasn't bluffing. Adam needed to know the extent of the damage that had been done to his stock and reputation. The more he knew, the better he could divert a scandal and the potential loss of millions of dollars.

An hour later, Ryan was emotionally exhausted. Dennis had called, as angry as she'd ever heard him, shouting threats about exposing her past and having her cut off from the family. He said everything but what she needed to hear, that he'd speak with Adam. He'd made his decision. She'd made hers—to expose the truth. Doing so may be the end of her family, but she had to do the right thing. She printed out the messages for Adam, then sent a text for them to meet ASAP about something important. She slipped on a pair of jeans, locked her door and had just pulled out of the garage when her cell phone rang. It was Bakersfield Medical.

She tapped the Bluetooth. "Hello?"

"Hi, may I speak to Ryan Washington?"

"This is Ryan."

"This is Kathy, a nurse at Bakersfield Medical. I'm working with the doctors who will be performing the transplant for your dad."

"Is something going on with Dad? Is he okay?"

"Your father's fine. I was rechecking your charts and noticed a trait that is genetic in nature. It won't impact the procedure. The surgery will go on as scheduled. But the doctor wondered if anyone had ever talked to you two about a specific gene, PCSK9?"

Ryan pulled over and put the car in Park. "What type of gene?"

"PCSK9. It manages the amount of cholesterol in the bloodstream. Those who do not have this gene or

have a mutation of it usually experience a lower cholesterol level and therefore are at less risk of heart disease. Total absence of the gene is quite rare, especially
in African Americans. The gene is not present in you
nor your father—"

"Wait, how can that be? I'm adopted."

There was a long pause on the other end of the line.

"I'm not sure what to tell you," the nurse finally said.
"This trait is passed along genetically, present in either
your mother or father. Are you in contact with your
birth parents, or do you have their medical records?"

"I need to make a phone call and get back with you."

Ryan hung up without saying goodbye, thoughts of
Adam and what she planned to share forgotten. Her fin-
gers were shaky as she punched another number. When
Ida answered, Ryan worked to find her voice.

"Is Joe Washington my birth father?" she managed.

Ida's hesitation was Ryan's answer. She walked into
the house as though through a fog, having learned the
biggest secret of all.

Twenty-One

"Hey, Chris." Adam stepped fully into Christian's office. "Do you have a minute?"

"I might." Christian was engrossed in something on the computer. He didn't look up. "Depends on what you need."

"A witness." That got Christian's attention. "The detective called me, says he has some information. He's in my office."

Christian was up before Adam finished his sentence. "Say no more. Let me close this out." A few taps on the keyboard, then he walked toward Adam. They left his office. "I'll be back in a bit," he told his secretary as they passed by her desk. "Unless it's an emergency, I'm unavailable."

Christian gave his brother a comforting pat on the shoulder. "Do you have any idea what you might hear?"

"Not a clue. But he's been on this for a month and it's the first time he requested a meeting."

"Then it must be something significant."

"I hope so. He's the top PI in the area and his rates reflect it."

Christian laughed. "I don't think he'll break your piggy bank."

Adam was appreciative of his brother's lightheartedness. Hearing from the detective had put a knot in his stomach. It felt more loose already. A look at his vibrating phone caused another smile. It was Ryan with a message about important, incredible news.

What happened last night? I was expecting you. Worried. Calls went to voice mail.

Sorry. Long story, need to tell you in person.

Headed to a meeting. Come by in an hour.

They walked into Adam's office. A guy of average height and medium build had been looking out the window. He turned when the two men walked in.

"Christian, this is Owen Haynes. Owen, this is my brother, Chris Breedlove."

They exchanged greetings.

"Let's sit over here, guys." Adam motioned toward a sitting area just around the corner of the large L-shaped corner office. Christian took a seat on a gray leather sofa. Owen chose one of two top-grain leather club chairs.

"Are you sure I can't get anything for you, Owen?"

"No, I'm good."

"All right, then." Adam sat on the other end of the couch. "What do you have for me?"

"Do you remember the commercial that asked, 'Where's the beef?'" At the confused look on both brothers' faces, he waved a dismissive hand. "Never mind. Too young. I can't answer the question of where the beef is, but I just might be onto who took it."

A slight ripple along the jaw Adam clinched was the only indicator of how tense he felt. His eyes slid to Christian, whose look was one of silent support.

Adam leaned forward. "I'm listening."

Owen pulled out a cell phone, tapped the face a few times then held it toward Adam.

"Do you recognize this guy?"

Adam took the phone and studied the picture on the screen. "This is out by the back gate."

Owen nodded. "It's time-stamped two thirty a.m."

Adam enlarged the picture, and saw boxes stacked up next to the gate and a man bent over them. A second guy carried a box to the truck, prime Wagyu no doubt. A baggy jumpsuit made it impossible to accurately guess the man's build and a baseball cap obscured his face.

"Ring any bells?" Owen asked.

"No," Adam said. "What about the guy by the fence? Did you get any of him?"

"Yes, but his whole face is covered, even the eyes. Swipe the screen. He's in the next couple pictures."

Adam's eyes narrowed as he studied the next few images. The second guy wore a baseball cap, sunglasses and a bandanna over his face. Totally unrecognizable, as Owen had said. *And likely the employee who's stealing.*

He scrolled back to the first picture and passed the phone to his brother. "Any idea who this is?"

Christian gazed at the screen for a moment, then shook his head. "I've never seen him before."

"What about the truck?" Owen asked.

"It doesn't look familiar. Send me those pictures. I'll have the parking lot cameras checked to see if it's ever been on the property."

"Dammit." Adam held out the cell phone. "I so want to catch whoever this is."

Owen forwarded the images to Adam, then pocketed the phone and stood. "Don't worry, there's a lot more video to study. These pictures are from the first one I downloaded and since one of the faces was fairly clear, I thought it was worth a shot to see if you recognized him. But I've got footage from here to the main highway in both directions. Learning who owns that truck and IDing the driver is just a matter of time."

"I appreciate the hard work," Adam said, standing up to shake Owen's hand.

"No problem, buddy. I'll be in touch." Owen tipped a well-worn cowboy hat to Christian before putting it on and walked out the door.

Christian placed a hand on Adam's shoulder. "Hang in there, bro."

Adam watched his brother exit, then crossed over to his desk. He downloaded the images from Owen and attached them to an email addressed to the head of security. He cc'd Stan, the ranch manager, then returned to the image of the truck with the boxes in the background, thieves in the very act of stealing the Wagyu that his men had so meticulously raised.

He sat back with the calm of a snake just before striking, confidently believing that it wasn't a matter of if he'd catch these guys, but when. His thoughts turned to Ryan, brightening his mood. After Owen's visit he could use a dose of her sunshine, and hoped whatever she had to share with him was good news.

Ryan pulled up to the valet counter, dread piercing the cloak of shock she'd worn since the fight with her brother and then, like a one-two punch, learning that Joe was her birth father. Ida had finally confirmed it. Dennis had texted more threats. Joe had called but Ryan hadn't answered. There was still too much to process. Plus, this wasn't a talk to have over the phone. She was headed to Bakersfield to see him in person, with one very important stop to make along the way. Everything about her life would change after that. Dennis would hate her. Adam would be angry. Ida might just kick her out of the clan. Her decision was risky but this was Vegas. Time to take a gamble and let the chips fall where they may.

It was Ryan's first visit to CANN's executive offices. Walking off the elevators was like entering another world, all gleaming and polished with the feel of wealth in the air. A deep, rich carpet soaked up any sound that her sandals may have caused as she crossed over to the receptionist desk. The perfectly coiffed woman on the other side made Ryan feel totally inadequate but the smile she offered helped to settle Ryan's nerves.

After the receptionist phoned Adam, they walked to a set of double doors at the end of a hallway. The receptionist motioned for Ryan to enter the office before quietly shutting the door.

Ryan stepped into what looked like a miniature lobby. "Adam?"

Hearing nothing, she ventured down an L-shaped hallway that opened into a room with a wall of glass, offering a breathtaking view of the strip to the north and the mountains to the west. Adam stood facing the mountains. He turned to her with a smile.

"There you are! I was on the phone. Hello, beautiful."

"Hey."

She walked into his outstretched arms and relished the warm embrace that he gave her. He kissed her. She allowed that, too, tried to return the fervor. The attempt was half-hearted. Her mind was too preoccupied.

Adam released her and stepped back. "Is everything okay? Are there problems with your father, with the transplant?"

"No, well, there has been a new development but Dad's okay. Everything is on course for the surgery to happen as scheduled."

"Then what's with the sadness that I detect in your voice?"

Ryan went to the window where Adam had stood. The view he had was picture-perfect. She was about to ruin it.

"Ryan," he softly coaxed. "What is it?"

"I know who's been stealing your product," she said, still taking in the view. Then she turned and faced him. "It's Dennis."

"Your brother?" She nodded. "Are you sure?"

"Positive."

Ryan watched Adam's face as he took in this information, saw the light dim from his eyes, the smile disappear from his face.

"Is that what you and Dennis were arguing about the other night at the plant?"

A slight pause and then, "Yes."

"Really?" Adam folded his arms across his chest. "How long have you known about this? Were you in on it, too?"

Ryan's shock was genuine, anger replacing fear of what she was disclosing and regret for not doing so sooner.

"How dare you! I come here to prove that my brother is stealing and you accuse me of betraying you? Fine." Ryan whirled around, then threw over her shoulder, "Get the proof on your own!"

She heard footsteps, then felt a strong hand on her arm.

"I'm sorry," Adam said. "But you lied to me, Ryan. I don't know what to believe."

"I never lied to you!"

"You did. That night when I walked in on you and Dennis arguing, I asked point-blank if either of you had anything you wanted to tell me. You could have shared this then, but you didn't."

"I still had no proof. It was my suspicions against his denials. He's my brother, Adam. I desperately wanted to believe what he told me, that he wasn't involved with what happened, that there was no fire behind the smoke. Not sharing my suspicions with you felt awful but the thought of accusing Dennis without being sure felt even worse."

"How long have you suspected him?"

"It started before the holidays, but—"

"The holidays?" Adam crossed over to where she stood by the window. "You've listened to my frustrations, rubbed away the kinks from the stress I've been under, and all this time knew who was behind it?"

"No! Aren't you listening? I had suspicions, a gut feeling, but nothing concrete. I questioned Dennis, told him how I felt. He repeatedly denied everything, said I was being paranoid. He even accused me of being jealous and wanting you all to myself."

Adam's eyes bore into her like lasers, almost black, the way they became in the throes of passion, now, with an emotion she couldn't comprehend.

"That night at my practice, when you shared what was happening, all of the suspicions I had flared up again. I became determined to find out the truth. And I did."

She reached into her purse. "This is what proved to me what Dennis is doing, text messages between him and Luke."

Adam exploded. "Luke was in on this, too? His so-called best friend was his partner in crime?"

He turned his back without taking the papers. Ryan's heart dropped. She placed a hand on his shoulder to offer comfort. He flinched, and shook it off.

"I'm sorry," she said, taking a step back to put space between them. "I don't blame you for being angry. Maybe I should have said something sooner."

He didn't turn around. She set the text message copies on a nearby table. "I'm telling you now because it's the right thing to do."

"You had suspicions this whole time but chose to remain silent, while I pulled out all the stops to catch this thief—more surveillance equipment, ID badges, security clearances, office renovations. All that, and I could have had the answer from you with just one phone call."

"He's my brother, Adam. I had to be sure. Can you forgive me?"

Adam crossed over to his desk and picked up his cell phone.

"Wait," Ryan said, closing the distance between them. "Aren't you going to say anything?"

"Yes," he said, slowly meeting her eyes. "Get out."

The command was low, raspy. Ryan hoped she'd misunderstood.

"What?" A whisper, barely pushed past the lump in her throat.

"You heard me."

"Okay, but have you heard me? Can't you understand how hard this was, the way going against my brother, my family, makes me feel?"

"Awful, I'm sure, the way I feel now, knowing I've spent time with a woman that I cannot trust."

Again he walked away from her, putting his massive oak desk between them. He sat down, his cell phone still in hand.

"Leave, Ryan, before I say something that can't be taken back. As for your question, in time, I might be able to forgive you. Until then, whenever that is, I don't want to hear from you again."

"You're angry, but, Adam, you can't mean that. I'm headed to—"

"I mean it." Adam's eyes blazed. "Do I need to call security or will you leave on your own?"

Ryan took one step back, then another. She turned, fleeing from his office. Outrunning her thoughts wasn't as easy. They chased her, taunting, as she hurried down the hallway.

Were you in on it, too?

Past the smiling receptionist.

The gene is not present in you nor your father, father, father...

To the elevator and through the lobby.

In time, I might be able to forgive you.

At the valet stand manned by the perky attendant.

Are you in contact with your birth parents?

In her car and a block away was the first time she became cognizant of breathing.

I don't want to hear from you.

Two blocks later the first tear fell. Before long there was a torrent sliding down her cheeks. It matched her flood of emotions—surprise, regret, sadness, disappointment and the merest, almost intangible feeling of joy. How could one of her best days also be one of her worst? She'd found one man, her birth father, but lost Adam Breedlove, the love of her life.

Twenty-Two

If you wronged one Breedlove, you wronged them all. So it was no surprise that a few days after Ryan's visit to Adam's office, Christian, Nick, Noah and their father had converged on the ranch to support Adam through the crisis. Detective Haynes was there, too, along with Clifford Dixon, the company's attorney, and Sasha Buchanan, a powerful and successful public relations fixer who'd been brought on board to handle damage control for Breedlove Beef's image, reputation and bottom line, as well as by association any spillover to CANN International. Owen had pored over extensive video footage and found pictures that pointed to Dennis being the masked man squatting near the boxes by the black truck, including one from a gas station with a clear image of Dennis getting into the truck, sans bandanna. Interestingly enough, though, it was Ryan's evidence that had given Adam the irrefutable proof needed to place the blame for what happened squarely on her brother. The legal team had acted swiftly and decisively, presenting a host of felony charges set to be filed. Dennis had one choice—cooperate fully or risk a long stint in jail, with his friend Luke likely there to keep him company. Dennis hadn't liked it, but the evidence was overwhelming. His attorney urged him to work out a deal before the courts got involved.

"Well, son," Nicholas asked once arrangements were finalized. "How do you feel?"

"Hopeful. I think the words coming directly from the culprit's mouth will help to clear mine and the company name. I'll know better after meeting with each affected customer face-to-face, to truly feel that I've regained their trust."

"I'm still concerned about one of the ways you're doing that, bro," Noah said. "Refunding 100 percent of all purchases to date, across the board, no questions asked, will cost you into the millions."

Typical Noah, Adam thought. Often considered aloof and impersonal, his brother was quiet, introspective, with an A-type personality that kept him focused, determined and single-minded. It's what made him a perfect team player in the financial arm of CANN International. But Noah could cut a person off as easily as breathing, could detach in a heartbeat. These traits contributed to his shrewd business dealings, but Adam thought it would make Noah a lifetime bachelor.

"Restoring one's reputation has no price," Adam finally told him.

"What about Ryan?" Christian asked.

"What about her?" Adam retorted.

"Come on, bro," Nick said. "Without those text messages, this thing might have dragged out in court for a very long time."

"I'll talk to Olivia," Adam said. "Have her send over something from the company."

Every Breedlove present gave him the eye before Nicholas spoke. "Whatever that young lady receives doesn't need to be prepared by your assistant or sent from the company. It needs to come from you."

Largely due to the respect Nevada and the food and service industry had for the Nicholas Breedlove, Sr., but also due to Adam's hard work and Sasha's top-notch PR, even in the face of some negative national coverage, the damage from the scandal was quickly contained. There was still a good two weeks between Adam and a full night's sleep, even longer for true peace of mind. But in at least one area of his life, things were turning back around. Adam had taken his daily horseback ride and had just stepped out of a long, hot shower when he heard the knocker. *Ryan.* He'd thought of her all week. It irked him that she was the first person who came to mind. After quickly slipping into a pair of jeans and pulling on a tee, walking down the hall and looking through the paned glass, he chided himself for feeling disappointed. He'd told Ryan to get out of his life. She'd done exactly as he'd asked.

He opened the door. "Hey, Mom."

"I was in the neighborhood and thought I'd drop by," Victoria said, a smile breaking through the concern on her face. "May I come in?"

"Of course." He stepped back so that she could enter, and noticed the ceramic pot she carried. "What's that?"

"Food," she said over her shoulder as she continued to the kitchen. "Which given how low those jeans are riding is clearly needed."

"I'm eating," he sullenly replied, though truth be told he couldn't remember the last meal.

Victoria set the pot on the stove, then turned to envelop him in a hug.

"I'm worried about you," she whispered as she stepped back and placed a hand on his cheek. "Though I must say, that beard makes you look rather debonair."

"Why are you worried?" Adam rounded the counter and slid onto a barstool. "I'm fine."

Victoria looked skeptical as she turned on the burner. "Not according to your brothers."

"My brothers have big mouths."

"And bigger hearts when it comes to their love for you. Christian was right. You haven't been sleeping. Those dark circles under your eyes are not cute."

Adam brushed a hand over his face as he slouched against the chair's back. "Yeah, trying to save a company, my reputation and the family name left little time for shut-eye."

"And little time for Ryan, from what I hear."

"Since the rest of the fam has kept you updated about the goings-on in my life, they had to have told you that Dennis's wasn't the only betrayal. That Ryan knew about what was going on and didn't say a word."

"They said she waited until she had proof." Victoria slowly stirred the creamy chicken and vegetable concoction. "And then passed that on to you."

"It was too little too late," Adam snapped.

"It was her brother," Victoria softly replied. "Did you thank her?"

Surely his mother was joking now. "For what?"

Victoria reached into the cabinet and pulled down a bowl, her voice gentle as she ladled soup into it.

"I cannot imagine the agony of knowing two men,

being related to one of them and very fond of the other, and having to make the hard choice of doing what's right, and noble, at great cost to that brother, and no doubt herself."

She placed the bowl in front of Adam. "Eat, son. You need your strength."

"You're not going to join me?"

"No, the soup smells delicious but my appetite seems to have scurried away." She walked around the counter, gave Adam a huge hug and a kiss on the cheek.

"You're a thoughtful man, Adam, a good man. I believe Ryan is a good woman. Whether or not you continue seeing her is none of my business. But I have a feeling she's had a pretty hard week, too, and probably without the type of support that you've enjoyed."

She squeezed his shoulder and turned to leave. Adam slid off the stool.

"Oh, no, sit and eat. I'll see myself out. Love you."

Adam watched the proud carriage of his mother until she turned the corner. He listened, heard the door gently shut. He took the spoon and stirred the soup, which indeed smelled delicious. But Victoria's words settled like a weight in his stomach. He couldn't eat a thing.

There was magic in Ryan's hands. Adam felt it all the way to the bone as she pulled and squeezed and worked the tension out of his body. She ran her fingers down the length of his spine before jiggling her bare bottom on his, and demanding he turn over. He did and beheld a goddess—gloriously naked—her breasts pert, nipples hard, hair wild and free.

She leaned down teasingly, her nipples brushing against his chest as she rained down light kisses. "I'm finished, lover," she purred. "Feel better?"

"Infinitely."

"Good. Now it's time for you to make me feel better, too."

She rose up then, her legs on each side of him, lovingly grasping his manhood, lining it up with the portal to paradise and sliding oh…so…slowly down.

Umm.

"Adam!"

"Yo, what?"

"You're over there snoring like a steam locomotive. You need to head to one of the bedrooms and get some real sleep."

Adam straightened and looked around, his mind dazed as he pulled himself from dream to reality. He was on the company plane, halfway through the list of customers to be visited. Instead of Ryan, it was his brother Nick beside him. Life wasn't fair.

"I'm good," he said, yawning, as he looked at his watch. "I've got a conference call with Earl soon, and need to prepare for it."

"That's not for another four hours, bro. You can't keep running on caffeine and conviction. You need real sleep. In a bed. For more than two hours."

"You're right." Adam motioned to the attendant and requested a double espresso.

Nick shook his head, tapping away on his satellite phone. "Fool."

Adam laughed, shamelessly peering over to view the profile pic on Nick's screen. "Is that Sasha?"

"Yes, why?"

"You're texting her?"

"Looks that way, doesn't it?"

"Is she back in Vegas?"

"Yes."

"Are you seeing her again?"

"No."

Adam peered at his brother. "Liar. I can't believe it. She dumped you, Nick. How could you let that woman back into your life?"

"How could you chase Ryan from yours?"

Adam didn't have a quick comeback for that.

"It's wrong how you're treating her," Nick added.

"There is no treating her one way or another. We broke up."

"That's the problem."

"No, the problem was her brother stealing and Ryan remaining quiet about it."

"With good reason. She had to be sure. That dude is her brother, man. Family first. You're tripping."

"No, you are, along with the rest of the fam. Ryan isn't the first woman I've stopped dating. If it doesn't bother me, it shouldn't bother you."

"That's why we keep bringing it up, Adam. Because the situation is bothering you, man. We all see it, we feel your unhappiness, and know it's not just about Breedlove Beef."

"Ryan was special, I'll admit that. But like you said, family first. Unfortunately, Dennis is a part of hers. How can there be a future with someone whose brother was stealing right under my nose?"

"Maybe there isn't one," Nick said, closing his eyes as he settled against the cushy seat. "But since you two are no longer dating, I guess we'll never know."

Adam sipped his espresso, bothered by Nick's uninvited opinions. Had Ryan spoken up sooner, the public scandal could have been avoided. He continued the internal argument but finally admitted the truth in the rebuttals his family presented. He and Ryan had unfinished business. It was time to give her a call.

Twenty-Three

Ryan had taken a few days off from her practice to try and recover from the secrets that had rocked her world—that the man she'd known for most of her life as her adopted father was her real dad, and that the brother she'd adored from childhood had stolen from the love of her life. She'd known all along that what she'd had with Adam was temporary, a fantasy. Still, the reality check hurt like hell.

Ryan's mother was still not speaking to her but she and her father texted every day. He kept her apprised of what was happening with Dennis, including news of an upcoming press conference that would be covered by local stations. Ryan idly surfed the channels looking for a distraction. But her mind kept returning to what happened a week ago when an innocent call and a firm rejection had changed her life.

* * *

Too upset to travel after meeting with Adam, Ryan had returned home and gone to bed, hoping a good night's rest would make life feel less awful. Sleep eluded her. At three forty-five she gave up trying, packed her car and hit the road. Four hours later she arrived in Bakersfield, shortly after her mother would have left for work. She reached her parents' home. April's mother helped to look after her dad and answered the door. Ryan told the kind neighbor that she'd take over watching her father. April's mother walked out the door. It was just Ryan and Joe now, alone. She walked up the stairs and knocked on the master bedroom door. There was no answer. She peeked in and saw her father, asleep. For a long moment, she stood at the end of the bed staring at him. Seeing his face as though for the first time, and traces of herself in it. He opened his eyes.

"I'm sorry, baby," he said, his voice raspy with sleep and emotion. "For years, I wanted to tell you but I gave Ida my word. I had you in my home. She had the secret. That was the deal."

Ryan sat on the bed and placed a hand on her father's arm. "You and Phyllis…"

"…had an affair. It shouldn't have happened but I'm not totally sorry because that's how we got you."

Joe talked for the next hour, almost nonstop. About how he, Phyllis, Ida and a group of others all used to be friends. He'd always been attracted to Phyllis but Ryan's birth mother wasn't into anything serious. She liked to party, liked adventure. Joe preferred a steady life and wanted a family. He married Ida, but Phyllis was still in his system. The affair was short, just a few weeks. But it only took one night to make a baby. The affair ended, but a new life had begun.

"Ida was livid," Joe continued. "And had every right. It was a betrayal of two friends, worse for me because I was also her husband. I didn't want to break up my family and did everything that Ida demanded. I cut all contact with Phyllis. Stayed true to my wife. It hurt to know about a child in the world, that I'd never seen, never touched. But I kept my word."

"But you found me, in foster care."

"That was Ida. The tough exterior she presents covers a heart of gold. As hurt as she was over what happened, she kept up with your whereabouts through mutual friends. Phyllis hurt her back and got hooked on pain pills. You went in the system. It took Ida a while to locate you and, while looking, she became a foster parent. When she found you, we took you in and gave you my name. It was Ida who did that, because a child needs her father. And while I never said anything to her about it, she knew this father needed his child."

It was an emotional discussion, one that taxed Joe's strength. He went to sleep and Ryan went to work on her father, hoping the energy healing provided some comfort or helped his rest. When Ida returned home, one look at Ryan's face and she knew that Joe had told her.

"Thank you," Ryan said simply, then walked to the woman she'd called Mom since being adopted and gave her the biggest hug. Ida stood there and slowly returned the embrace. When the hug ended, there were tears in both of their eyes. They sat at the table and had a long conversation, for Ryan, the best one ever. They cooked and cared for Joe, talked to the doctors, made plans for the transplant. She'd lost Adam but still had her fam-

ily. The hope that they'd survive this ordeal grew with
each passing hour.

Then Dennis came home. The peace was shattered.
He blamed Ryan for everything. Ida took Dennis's side.
Joe was too weak to weigh in. Ryan returned to Las
Vegas ready for the surgery, but unsure of everything
else.

"There is breaking news this hour regarding Breedlove Beef and the controversy surrounding the low
grades of meat some customers received instead of the
high-quality Wagyu they'd ordered. Let's go live to a
press conference happening now."

The voice from the television drew Ryan's attention
back to the screen, where her brother stood at a podium.
He looked terse and uncomfortable, as he read from a
prepared statement.

"My name is Dennis Washington. A few months
ago I was hired as the manager for the Breedlove Beef
Processing Center in Breedlove, Nevada, by the owner,
Adam Breedlove. I abused the authority and access I
had to the facility to engage in practices that were unethical and caused great damage to the Breedlove name
and the company brand. I take full responsibility for any
product delivered to any person or company that was
not what they ordered, or expected. I exploited our prior
friendship and Adam's good name for personal gain.
He knew nothing of what I was doing. For that, as well
as the harm done to him and his family, I apologize."

Ryan had seen enough. She reached for the remote,
but was stopped by the next face that appeared on the
screen. Adam. Her heart raced. She leaned forward, taking him in as if it had been years instead of days since
she'd seen him. He was surrounded by reporters yet

appeared relaxed, managing to smile despite the tough topic. Even though his angular face was sharper than she remembered, as though he'd lost weight, the camera loved him. Ryan did, too. Which was probably why she spent more time than she should wondering about the gorgeous woman standing just behind Adam, along with what she assumed were execs from the ranch. In all the coverage watched or read there'd been no mention of charges or jail time for Dennis, and no mention of Luke at all. Time would tell if Ryan's hunch was correct, that even when wronged Adam could be the bigger, better man. Instinctively, she picked up the phone to call him. But memories of his parting words stilled her fingers. Adam had moved on. When her phone rang a short time later with the name Victoria on her Caller ID, Ryan couldn't have been more surprised.

"This is Ryan."

"Hello, Ryan. It's Victoria."

"Hi, Victoria."

"How are you, sweetheart?"

Her interest seemed genuine. Ryan was floored. "Okay, I guess. Busy."

"Then I won't keep you. I'm following up on the call I made a while back and the information regarding our event that my assistant sent you. Did you get it?"

"Not that I remember. It may have gone to spam." As for the call received in what felt like a lifetime ago, Ryan had forgotten it until now. "I'm sorry, there's been a lot going on."

"I can only imagine how difficult this time has been for you, which is why I hope you'll forgive my extreme presumption in placing you on the program for our affair. You don't have to attend, of course, but I wish you would."

As Victoria talked, Ryan scrolled through emails and found an unread one from the CANN Foundation. It explained that Integrative Healing had been listed on the program and Victoria would love it if she could attend. Ryan was very surprised, and grateful. She asked a few more questions and then told Victoria she'd most definitely be there.

Ryan arrived early, per Victoria's request, ready to offer the services of massage and Reiki energy healing to as many of the one hundred women in attendance as she could. There'd been so many surprises about that day, starting with the fact that Victoria had not canceled her appearance, that she'd invited her even after what happened with Adam.

"You two still haven't talked?" Victoria asked, as they walked from the foundation offices to the ball-room.

"No. I'm pretty sure that's not going to happen."

"Breedlove men are very proud and when angered, or hurt, can be very stubborn. What you did was honorable and courageous, and I applaud your actions. They told me that you're exactly the type of young lady that those attending this charitable event need to see."

Victoria was the only person besides Brooklyn who'd agreed with her actions. Ryan didn't know what to say.

"How's your family handling all this? There must be friction."

"To put it mildly," Ryan said, the understatement producing a smile. "My dad's been in touch, keeping me updated. They're grateful that Adam didn't press charges that would have likely sent Dennis to prison. But neither him nor my mother is speaking to me."

"Stay encouraged," Victoria said, placing an arm around her. "When it comes to family, we never give up."

They entered the elaborately decorated ballroom to more surprises. Ryan had expected to see well-heeled women wearing their favorite designers and enough diamonds to cancel the national debt. Some of the women indeed fit this description but others, though nicely dressed, were clearly out of their element. Victoria explained that every donor had purchased two tickets, one for themselves and one to be donated to a woman of lesser means. Victoria wanted them to experience a little bit of luxury, to be treated like queens for the day.

With everything set up, Ryan thought it would be a good time to run to the restroom. She'd just begun to head that way when Victoria waved her over.

"Are we ready to start?" Ryan asked.

"Yes, lunch will begin in about twenty minutes."

"I thought that was happening after the show."

"No, the fashion show takes place as the women are eating. You didn't read the email?"

"Not entirely," Ryan sheepishly replied.

"You're forgiven. Listen, I waved you over because I need your help. There's someone we've invited who's just a little nervous about this whole affair. She's in one of our smaller dining rooms and I thought if you could go in and work some of your magic, she'll feel more comfortable coming out."

"Oh, of course. I'd be glad to help. Where is she?"

They walked out of the main ballroom and down a hall where smaller, private dining rooms were located. "She's in the last room on the right." Victoria's phone rang. "I've got to get back."

"Oh, Victoria…"

But she was gone. Ryan wished she'd gotten the woman's name. But it didn't matter. Once treatment began, her body would tell Ryan all she needed to know.

Ryan gave a soft knock, and then opened the door.

"Hello," she said softly, as she stepped inside.

"Hi, Ryan."

Ryan froze before slowly turning around and coming face-to-face with her birth mom.

"What…are you doing here?"

"Don't be mad," Phyllis said, her eyes searching Ryan's face. "That lady, Victoria, asked me and Ida to come here. Ida couldn't make it but she called me, the first time we talked in years. She said that Joe told you everything. She told me about the transplant, too, and you giving him a kidney. The best part is that she finally forgave me, Ryan, and if you will have me she gave me her blessing to be in your life."

Twenty-Four

Ryan pulled into a parking space at the far end of the Strip, turned off her car and walked toward the sign with deep blue coloring and white lettering bearing her name. In the days since all of the secrets were revealed, and all the lives that they had affected were being mended, Ryan had finally allowed someone long denied a voice—the little girl inside her. The inner child who from a very early age had longed for her real mother. She placed a key in the lock and stepped into the interior painstakingly designed to bring peace to those who entered, a thought that was bittersweet because missing Adam denied her that serenity.

A tinkling bell signaled the inner door opening. Brooklyn walked into the foyer. "Ryan!" She rushed over and gave her a hug.

"Come on, I just made tea and don't have an appointment for another thirty minutes." They began walking toward the back and the mini kitchen. "Needless to say I've been very concerned about you."

"I'm sorry to have worried you."

"No apology needed. I saw your brother's press conference. When you left the message about canceling clients and taking time off, I thought it was a wise thing to do."

Brooklyn busied herself making the tea. For several seconds, Ryan watched her, realizing that the woman she considered to be her best friend knew almost nothing about her past. Brooklyn finished dressing the tea and handed her a steaming mug.

"Okay, sit," Brooklyn commanded, in a voice that was soft yet firm. Ryan pulled a chair away from the quaint bamboo table and sat down. Brooklyn took the seat next to her. "Talk."

Ryan hesitated, but only briefly. "I'm adopted."

Brooklyn nodded. "I had a feeling that you were."

"Your intuition?" Ryan asked.

"I guess so."

"I should have known."

"That time you told me about a client looking for her parent, I had a gut feeling it might have been you." Brooklyn smiled, and squeezed Ryan's arm. "It's okay."

"I know that now, but for twenty years that was a secret I felt forced to keep."

Brooklyn set down her cup. "Hang on a minute, I'll be right back."

"I shouldn't—"

"No, you're fine. I just need to grab my phone."

Ryan waited, sipped her tea, amazed at how much a lie could weigh and how much lighter she felt since learning the truth surrounding her birth.

"Okay, I'm all yours."

"But your clients?"

Brooklyn waved a dismissive hand. "I just silenced the ringer. Besides, right now, you're more important."

Ryan shared everything about what had happened that culminated with Ryan seeing her biological and adoptive mothers together for the very first time.

"All of us were suffering individually," she finished. "Afraid of a bogeyman created in our minds. There's still a lot of work to do, and we'll probably never go on a girls' trip, but we realized there's room to be civil. My birth mom Phyllis understands that Mom isn't the devil, and Mom understands that Phyllis isn't a threat. I never thought this day would come."

"I'm so glad it did." Brooklyn leaned over and hugged Ryan. "What about Adam? How does he feel about it?"

Ryan sighed, realizing that even with the bomb she'd dropped about being adopted, there was another explosive topic to deal with.

"You watched Dennis's press conference, right?"

"Yes, but I didn't really understand the apology."

When Ryan finished the short version of what had happened a few minutes later, all Brooklyn could say was "Wow."

"I know. It's like I've been trapped in a really bad movie and can't get out."

"You love Adam! What are you going to do?"

Ryan shrugged. "I've reached out to him. He hasn't called back, but he knows how I feel. Right now, I'm focusing on Dad and the upcoming surgery. I can't live in the past."

Brooklyn's phone buzzed with a call she had to take. Ryan reheated her tea and walked into the office she hadn't seen in a week. She hadn't planned on working but now didn't want to leave. So she retrieved her laptop from the car, fired it up and within two hours had rescheduled the clients from the past several days, giving a discount for the inconvenience her unexpected absence had caused them. She called the web designer and discussed ideas for her upcoming blog. Life lessons were never only for the person who learned them. She knew there were other adoptees out there navigating the sensitive waters flowing between the moms who birthed them and the moms who raised them. Too many families kept too many secrets, leaving wounds sometimes not recognized and scars that never healed. As she finished up the notes on what she wanted to send over, her phone rang.

Dennis.

What did he want? He was back at their parent's home in Bakersfield. How could she help him? A favor perhaps? Something to ask her ex-lover and his former boss? She let the call go to voice mail. Adam was currently not speaking to her, and with Dennis there was no more to say.

The week passed quickly. Ryan tried to embrace her new normal. Work helped. The pavement-pounding, networking and social media presence was paying off, along with referrals and repeat business. Learning that Joe was her birth dad had filled her heart with more love than she thought she could hold. Still, she missed Adam with every breath. It was crazy to believe he'd contact her after everything Dennis had done and how he felt she'd betrayed him. She tried to not think about him, to bury her emotions beneath a pile of paperwork and scheduling screens. Just when she'd managed almost an hour without a thought about Adam, he called.

"This is Ryan."

"Hello, Ryan. It's Adam."

"Hi."

"I got your messages but have been out of the country. I'm still out, but will be back on Saturday."

"I thought you might still be upset with me."

"I'm not angry with you, Ryan. Not anymore. What happened wasn't your fault."

"At times it felt that way." Ryan's honesty was met with silence. "Adam?"

"I should have contacted you sooner," he said. "My schedule's been crazy. How are you?"

"I'm okay."

"Ryan, what else did you want to share that day you came to my office? I was so angry at the news about Dennis that I couldn't hear anything else."

"I've tried to put myself in your shoes and can somewhat understand you being so upset."

"Still, it was wrong of me to cut you off that day without hearing everything you wanted to tell me. I'd like to have that chance again."

"I don't know, Adam. It's probably not necessary. What we had is over and—"

"You still deserve to be heard. It wasn't until my schedule slowed down that I remembered part of your text mentioned having incredible news. What did you want to tell me?"

"I'm adopted and have been looking for my birth father. The day I came to your office, I'd found him."

Ryan told Adam about her childhood, about finding and building a relationship with her birth mom, Phyllis, and what she'd learned of her dad.

"You've dealt with a lot. I'm proud of you, Ryan. You sound really happy."

"I am. No more secrets. It's good to not hide it any-more."

"It also solves a puzzle that I couldn't figure out," Adam responded.

"What?"

"How you can be such an angel while Dennis is the devil in disguise."

They shared a laugh, reminding Ryan of the easy ca-maraderie that used to exist between them and making her wonder if they could ever get it back.

"I've been very selfish."

"Why do you say that?"

"Since the scandal broke, my complete focus was on the business and how I'd been affected. I was too angry to consider what you'd gone through, more than I ever suspected. While crisscrossing the globe to meet clients, I've had time to reflect on the whole situation and the strength it took to do what you did. I treated you unfairly, Ryan. I'm sorry."

"It's okay."

"No, it's not. I'm a better man than the one you've seen recently. I've missed you terribly and if given the opportunity, I'll do everything I can to make it up to you. Will you forgive my past actions and give me that chance, Ryan? I didn't mean what I said that day at the office. Will you see me again?"

"Of course," Ryan managed, while fighting back tears. "I appreciate the kind words but just so you know, life's been pretty miserable without you, too."

"Then let's end the misery for both of us. I'll call you as soon as I land."

"Sounds good."

"There's one more thing."

"What?"

"I love you, Ryan."

Ryan hadn't expected the *L* word but answered from her heart.

"I love you, too."

Twenty-Five

A few months later

Adam took one last look around the en suite bath, then returned to his bedroom. He closed the top of the carry-on luggage that rested on the bed, zipped it up and reached for the phone he'd tossed next to it earlier. Seconds later, a groggy voice answered the phone.

"Adam?"

"Good morning, Ryan."

"What time is it? Is everything okay?"

"Everything's fine. Look, I've got something cool to show you. A car is on the way to pick you up."

"Now?" He could hear what sounded like her moving around, perhaps getting out of bed.

"I know it's early but if we're going to do all that I've planned, we have to start now. Don't worry. I've taken care of everything. You're spending the night. So throw a few toiletries in a bag and dress comfortably. Elvis will be there in about thirty minutes."

"What if I said I didn't want to come over?"

"Then I'd have to come kidnap you."

"I appreciate that, babe, but there's a reason I didn't plan anything this weekend. I'm really exhausted and just want to chill out."

"Then that's exactly what we'll do. Now, please, go get ready. Elvis will be there soon."

Adam ended the call, pulled the luggage to the floor and rolled it behind him as he left the room. Passing by the counter he picked up his keys, phone and sunglasses and continued out of the house to the wraparound porch. He stopped and put on his shades, taking a moment to breathe in the smell of freshly cut grass and to appreciate the cool morning breeze. The day was new and fresh, like his relationship with Ryan.

Adam couldn't wait to see her reaction to the plans he'd made. Her happiness meant everything, a fact that Adam found quite surprising given the chain of events that had led his heart there. Dennis Washington had cost him a chunk of money for a scheme that could have caused his business to fail before hardly getting started. Still, Adam could never hate his former friend. Knowing him is how he'd met Ryan. Since that Sunday when they'd reconnected, their love had blossomed. For that, he'd do it all again.

He crossed over to where a profusion of colors burst from the aspen trees he'd had planted for that very reason—because of how their leaves changed in fall. Shades of red and orange and yellow were highlighted, backlit by the sun. The leaves actually looked happy and free, the way that he felt since admitting his struggles with dyslexia to a business blogger. The article went viral. Adam became an inspiration for others who struggled, proof that the challenge could be overcome. Owning that truth allowed him to fit fully and comfortably inside his own skin and realize that others knowing about his disability made him no less of the person he'd been before that truth came out. This realization and newfound appreciation for authenticity would have never happened except for Ryan. Meeting that woman had changed his life in so many ways. He hoped to return the favor.

Adam heard the sound of a car. He turned to see the executive SUV he'd sent to pick up Ryan coming down the drive. He strolled over to where he'd left his luggage and, after making sure the door had been locked, headed toward the drive. Once the car had pulled in and parked, the driver quickly exited the car.

Adam waved him away. "Thanks, Elvis, but I've got it."

"You sure?"

"Positive. Hey," he quickly continued, motioning for Elvis to come toward him. "You didn't tell her, did you?"

"She doesn't know a thing," Elvis replied with a wink.

Adam placed his luggage in the back, then opened the door and climbed inside. Ryan sat cross-legged, her back against the door, looking as fit as a fiddle. Not at all like someone with only one kidney.

"I thought we were just going to hang out" was her *good morning*.

"We are."

"Then why are you getting in the car?"

"To take us to where we're hanging out." Adam

stretched his body over the seat for a quick kiss. "Good morning, gorgeous!"

"You woke me out of a deep sleep and had me picked up before breakfast, even coffee. We'll see how good it is."

Adam took in her black skinny jeans, sweater and faux leather jacket. Her face was devoid of makeup, and the hair that often had a mind of its own was held away from her face with a band. She looked adorable.

"I didn't bring a change of clothes."

"You look fine."

"But you brought a suitcase. Where are we going?"

"Just relax, Ryan. Since you're a business owner, I know you are keen on the details and like to be in control. For today, let taking care of you be my job. Okay?"

He kissed her once, and again, and watched the pout she'd worn slip away. "Okay." She looked out the window. "I can't get over the beauty of this estate. It's like being in a whole other world."

"In many ways, it is. Mom wanted to create a type of fantasyland for family, guests and clientele. With every renovation or new edition, she outdoes herself."

Ryan looked over at him. "What were some of the changes?"

The car stopped. "I'll answer that question after we get on the plane."

"Plane? Adam, where are we going?"

"Not far. I'll get your door." Long strides made quick work of covering the distance. "Come on, babe."

"No." Ryan crossed her arms. "I refuse to go where I don't know where I'm going!"

"Ha!" He held out his hand. "Do you trust me? Well, do you?"

She gave him the side-eye but placed her hand in

his and allowed herself to be pulled out of the car. In the meantime Elvis had retrieved Adam's luggage. Still holding Ryan's hand, Adam grabbed the luggage handle and led them toward the plane.

"Thanks, Elvis!"

They reached the airstairs of a private plane. Ryan looked up. "We're going in that?"

"Yes, isn't it a beauty? Come on."

Adam entered the plane and stopped near the cockpit, where the pilot and flight attendant were standing. He introduced Ryan.

"Nice meeting you, young lady," the pilot said. "Check's all done, Adam. We can take off anytime."

Adam gave him a thumbs-up. "Let's go!"

He stopped at the first set of seats. "Aisle or window?"

"Window." He stepped back so Ryan could pass him, watched her eyes scan the plane's interior, which even after all the times he'd flown in it was still impressive.

"Buckle up, babe."

Ryan reached for the belt, still looking around. Her eyes landed on a shiny plaque. "Christian Breedlove, President, CANN International." She looked at Adam. "Ah, so this is the company's plane?"

Adam shook his head. "It belongs to Christian, a birthday gift from our parents."

"Wow. Mom and Dad gave Dennis a toy plane one Christmas but...oops, sorry."

Adam laughed. "Don't worry about it. He's still your brother."

He pulled Ryan into his arms as the plane barreled down the runway and began its ascent. There was a companionable silence as the two looked out the window, first at clouds and blue sky and then at mountains bathed in different hues once the plane leveled out. Angie, the attendant, walked out carrying an ornate silver tray holding two flutes, a basket of miniature rolls, a covered dish and a small bouquet of perfectly formed roses.

"It's only an hour flight but this will get you started," Angie said.

"Can I help you?" Adam asked.

"Oh, no. I've got it." She pulled down a tabletop from the wall in front of them and put down the tray. "I've got coffee on as well and there is hot chocolate available, along with champagne if you'd like to turn that juice into a mimosa. What else can I bring you?" She looked from Adam to Ryan.

"Hot chocolate sounds good," Ryan said.

Adam nodded. "Make that two."

Ryan leaned forward and pulled one of the roses from the bouquet. She touched it to her nose and deeply inhaled. "This smells amazing. I've never smelled a rose this fragrant, or seen one this big. These are huge! I also don't think I've ever seen an orange rose."

She placed the flower to her nose again, looking at Adam with love in her eyes. "Were these brought on board just for me?"

"Absolutely." Adam reached for the two flutes. He gave one to Ryan. "To celebrate the woman who's touched my life and captivated my heart. This day is for you."

"That's so sweet, babe." Ryan gave Adam a quick kiss on the lips before they clinked glasses and took sips. "Thank you. What's under the dome?"

Adam raised the silver top to reveal two beautifully plated servings of eggs Florentine.

"Yum!"

He reached for one of the small plates and handed it to Ryan, then picked up the other and began eating.

"How's Joe doing?" he asked, and was immediately rewarded with one of her life-giving smiles.

"Dad's recovery is amazing. The first couple weeks were scary. We didn't know whether or not his body would accept my kidney. With the time that's passed the doctors are increasingly optimistic. They've even made plans to visit…"

"What?"

"Never mind."

"Is it about Dennis? Baby, I've made my peace with what he did. I lost all of the trust and respect I had for him, and he'll never again work in the meatpacking industry, or any part of the service industry, most likely. But I don't hate your brother."

"I appreciate that," Ryan said. "The way he was treated in Bakersfield after the press conference was worse than being in jail. A month ago he got engaged to the neighbor and moved to Texas with her and her kids. My parents will visit him soon."

"And you?"

Ryan shook her head. "I'm still working on forgiving him for the pain he's caused me. Not just what he did to you but from the time I was adopted. I don't hate Dennis, either, but I honestly can't say I like him much right now."

"Then have Brooklyn do some of that woo-woo stuff to help you heal. Unforgiveness hurts only you."

"Woo-woo stuff?" Ryan laughed. "Listen to you! But you're right. I tell my clients that all the time and need to take your advice."

They chatted about the past week's events and raved about the food. Angie returned with their hot chocolate, and to refill their flutes. Shortly after they'd finished eating, she returned for their dishes and picked up the tray.

"We'll be landing shortly," she said. "Time to buckle up."

Ryan looked out the window. "This isn't Los Angeles," she said, stretching her neck this way and that. "Are we going to Phoenix?"

"A few more minutes and the destination will be revealed."

The plane landed and the captain announced, "Welcome to Sedona."

"Babe! I love Sedona!" As she turned and threw her arms around his neck, the brightness of Ryan's eyes and smile were enough to add years to his life.

"We'd better get out of these seats and get to it, then."

Ryan released the belt and stood. "How did you know?"

"I talked to Brooklyn. She told me this was one of your favorite spots."

They said goodbye to the crew and walked down the stairs to a waiting car. Once inside, Ryan reached for his arm. "This is really special. Thanks again."

"You're very welcome."

"Did Brooklyn tell you anything about Sedona? There's lots to do here depending on what you're in the mood for, and places where we can eat later on. Ooh, babe, had I known we were coming here I would have worn different clothes!"

"Don't worry, gorgeous," he replied. "You're the most beautiful woman in town. Now—" he pulled her into a gentle embrace "—tell me about Sedona and why you love it."

"It's beautiful, for one thing," Ryan said, resting her

head against his arm and sounding dreamy. "It feels good and when I come here, no matter what my mood is beforehand, I soon feel good, too. It's because of the vortexes, these pockets of energy that can heal and transform. People come from all over the world to experience them. It's pretty cool."

They chatted a bit more, him asking questions, Ryan answering them, until they pulled into an über-luxurious hotel and spa called, appropriately, Vortex.

"Unbelievable," Ryan whispered with an almost childlike wonder. "This place has been on my bucket list for years!"

"Brooklyn said I'd score points by bringing you here."

"My bestie was right. You. Are. Winning!"

Adam had grown up in luxury, but from the lobby to their penthouse suite, he was impressed. Ryan was overwhelmed. He'd wanted her to feel like Cinderella and had pulled out all the stops. They toured the town, attended a festival and took a ride in a hot air balloon. When they returned to the car, Ryan nestled against him. "I'm so deliriously happy right now."

Adam kissed her temple as he placed an arm around her. "Have I worn you out yet?"

"I'm strangely invigorated," she murmured, placing a hand on his thigh while looking at him coyly, a clear message in her eyes.

He gently gripped her hand, stopping its movement toward his crotch. "I've had that on my mind since we got on the plane," he admitted. "But later, after dinner, when I can take my time and—" he ran a finger down her face, neck and the top of her breast "—do things right."

"After dinner, huh?" Adam nodded. "Can we make it quick, like go through a drive-through?"

"Ha!"

When they arrived back at the hotel, Ryan was shocked to see a closet filled with shoeboxes and clothes, courtesy of a designer Victoria had recommended. He'd had every clothing item delivered that a woman needed, from lingerie to Louboutins.

"Baby, you've thought of everything. You've turned me into a big crybaby with all of these gifts!"

"I don't mind. I'm just happy you like them."

"I love them," Ryan responded. "I love you."

They showered—separately, amid Ryan's protestations—and went to dinner dressed to the nines. Adam's tailored umber-colored suit shot through with gold thread made him look dashing and complemented Ryan's shimmery, one-shoulder silk delight that hugged her curves the way Adam planned to later. The menu was a symphony of vegetables, grains, starches and legumes that created gastronomic melodies over olfactory harmonies so good that Ryan requested the chef be brought to their table and thanked in person.

Ryan reached over for Adam's hand. "You know, babe, I think this might be the best day in my entire life."

"Really?"

"Definitely. You're an amazing man, Adam Breedlove. It's seems such an inadequate statement given all you've done, but thank you, for everything."

"You're welcome, babe, but the night's not over."

"Oh, I know that," she said, her voice flirty and low.

Adam chuckled. "Are you ready?"

"Sure."

They walked out of the restaurant. She headed toward the elevator. He caught her arm and began walking toward the exit.

"Where are we going?"

"My last treat of the day."

"What else is left to do?"

"You'll see."

The same car that had driven them around all day idled in the circular drive. The driver stood by the opened car door and nodded slightly as they entered. Adam immediately pushed a button to raise the privacy screen and pulled a more-than-willing Ryan into his arms. He slid his tongue along the crease of her mouth as a finger tickled her nipple. She gasped, providing the opening he wanted. His tongue darted inside her mouth, touching the tip of hers, which eagerly awaited to touch, taste, dance together.

When Ryan's hand once again crept toward Adam's burgeoning erection, he put on the brakes.

"Babe, if you let the snake out of the cage we won't reach our destination."

"Releasing that snake is my destination," she whispered against his mouth. "But I'll behave."

The car turned off the highway onto a dirt road that ran along the edge of a mountain. It was a cool, clear evening, almost dark, and the higher the car climbed the brighter the stars shone.

"It's so beautiful out here," Ryan whispered, almost reverently. "I can't imagine where you're taking me, though."

"To heaven, I hope," Adam replied.

The car pulled over. Adam instructed the driver to open the trunk. "Wait here," he said to Ryan. He retrieved items from the trunk and returned to the car.

Once inside he handed Ryan a large cashmere shawl. "It's bit chilly out," he told her.

"You've thought of everything," she said.

"I try." He reached into a large canvas bag in the trunk and pulled out a pair of slip-on sneakers. "I love those stilettos but these will work better on the mountain."

"I love being out here in all of this beauty, but, babe, I'm not exactly dressed for a hike."

"What I'd like to show you isn't far and won't take long." He removed his suit jacket and donned a pullover sweater. "You ready?"

"Sure."

Adam stepped out of the car, hoisted the bag on his shoulder and reached back in for Ryan. There was a blanket of stars across a clear, dark sky; some seemed almost low enough to touch. Adam held Ryan securely as they followed the rocky trail going up the mountain until the path opened up onto a wide plateau. From here they couldn't see the car or the road. Rock formations isolated them from everything, created a world with Ryan and Adam only, no one else. Ryan stepped away from Adam, dropped her head back and spun around. Her eyes landed on an object a short distance away. She walked over and squealed.

"A telescope!"

Hurriedly, she put her eye to the lens. "Wow, this is amazing. There's the Big Dipper," she said, while swiveling the machine in different directions. "And there's the North Star. Babe, you've got to see this. It's like I really am in heaven and can catch these stars in the palm of my hand."

Adam took a turn to look in the telescope. After a while he turned to her. "Ryan, I think you're right."

"What?"

"The stars. They're so close. I believe we can catch them, too." He walked over to Ryan. "Hold out your hand."

Ryan cocked her head. "It was a figure of speech, Adam. Even if a star fell, which they really don't, having it land in my hand would be a long shot, even for a Breedlove."

"Everything is possible," he responded. "That's what the woman at the festival who worked with crystals said." He paused, stepped closer and looked deeply into her eyes. "Do you believe that's true?"

"Yes."

"Good. Hold out your hand and close your eyes."

Ryan's eyes slowly closed as her hand lifted.

"Now, make a wish upon a star and ask it to come to where you are." He waited. "Abracadabra," he slowly said, releasing what he'd pulled from his pocket and letting it fall.

Ryan jumped as she felt an object hit her hand. She opened her eyes and saw something sparkling, a ring with so many carats that it shone brighter than Polaris or any of the other stars. Her eyes slowly raised from the ring to Adam's face, glimmering with unshed tears.

"What's this?" she whispered.

He picked up the dazzling princess-cut rock set in platinum and held it between his fingers. "It's not a falling star," he said, "but it represents my wish for us. My world hasn't been the same since you entered it. Everything's brighter. I'm a better person, a better man. I might not be able to give you the world or even a planet, but I can give you my heart."

Adam watched a single tear slide down Ryan's cheek

as he got down on one knee. "Will you marry me, Ryan, and fulfill all my wishes?"

"Yes," she said after a pregnant pause, where her lips trembled and she composed herself. "Because you just made all of mine come true."

Adam stood and pulled Ryan into his arms. They kissed with passion and desire amid a shower of falling stars. Adam had fallen for the vegetarian practitioner. Ryan was ready for the cattle-raising rancher. Together, they planned to weave those differences into a lifetime of harmonious love.

* * * * *

#2695 RANCHER'S WILD SECRET

Gold Valley Vineyards • by Maisey Yates

Holden McCall came to Gold Valley with one goal: seduce his enemy's innocent engaged daughter, Emerson Maxfield. But the tempting cowboy didn't plan for good girl Emerson to risk everything, including her future, to indulge the desire neither can resist...

#2696 HOT HOLIDAY RANCHER

Texas Cattleman's Club: Houston • by Catherine Mann

Rancher Jesse Stevens wants to get married, but Texas heiress Esme Perry is *not* the woman the matchmaker promised. And when they're stranded together during a flash flood—over Christmas—will passion sweep them into something more than a holiday fling?

#2697 THE REBEL

Dynasties: Mesa Falls • by Joanne Rock

Lily Carrington is doubly off-limits to Marcus Salazar: not only is she engaged to another man when she meets the media mogul, but she's also a spy for his business-rival brother. Can Marcus tame his desire for her—and will he want to?

#2698 A CHRISTMAS RENDEZVOUS

The Eden Empire • by Karen Booth

After a chance encounter leads to a one-night stand, lawyers Isabel Blackwell and Jeremy Sharp find themselves reunited on opposite sides of a high-stakes case at Christmas. As their forbidden attraction reignites, her past and a surprise revelation threaten everything...

#2699 SECOND CHANCE TEMPTATION

Love in Boston • by Joss Wood

Years ago, Tanna left Boston businessman Levi at the altar. Now she's back to make amends and move on with her life. Until Levi traps her into staying—and shows her the life she could have had. But their complicated past could destroy their second chance...

#2700 ONE NIGHT, TWO SECRETS

One Night • by Katherine Garbera

Heiress Scarlet O'Malley *thinks* she had a one-night stand with a certain Houston billionaire, but learns it was his twin, Alejandro Velasquez! The switch isn't her only shock. With a baby on the way, can their night of passion last a lifetime?

———————

Get 4 FREE REWARDS!

We'll send you 2 FREE Books <u>plus</u> 2 FREE Mystery Gifts.

Harlequin® Desire books feature heroes who have it all: wealth, status, incredible good looks... everything but the right woman.

FREE
Value Over
$20

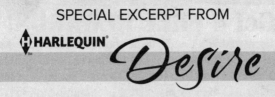
"I'll tell you what," he said. "I'm going to give you a kiss.
And if afterward you can walk away, then you should."

She blinked. "I don't want to."

"See how you feel after the kiss."

He dropped the ax, and it hit the frozen ground with a
dull thump.

He already knew.

He already knew that he was going to have a hard time
getting his hands off her once they'd been on her. The
way that she appealed to him hit a primitive part of him
he couldn't explain. A part of him that was something
other than civilized.

She took a step toward him, those ridiculous high
heels somehow skimming over the top of the dirt and
rocks. She was soft and elegant, and he was half-dressed

and sweaty from chopping wood, his breath a cloud in the cold air.

She reached out and put her hand on his chest. And it took every last ounce of his willpower not to grab her wrist and pin her palm to him. To hold her against him, make her feel the way his heart was beginning to rage out of control.

He couldn't remember the last time he'd wanted a woman like this.

And he didn't know if it was the touch of the forbidden adding to the thrill, or if it was the fact that she wanted his body and nothing else. Because he could do nothing for Emerson Maxfield, not Holden Brown, the man he was pretending to be. The man who had to depend on the good graces of his employer and lived in a cabin on the property. There was nothing he could do for her.

She didn't even want emotions from him.

But this woman standing in front of him truly wanted only this elemental thing, this spark of heat between them to become a blaze.

And who was he to deny her?

Will their first kiss lead to something more than either expected?

Find out in
Rancher's Wild Secret
by New York Times *bestselling author Maisey Yates.*

Available November 2019 wherever
Harlequin® Desire books and ebooks are sold.

Harlequin.com

Love Harlequin romance?

DISCOVER.

Be the first to find out about promotions,
news and exclusive content!

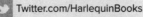 Facebook.com/HarlequinBooks

Twitter.com/HarlequinBooks

Instagram.com/HarlequinBooks

Pinterest.com/HarlequinBooks

ReaderService.com

EXPLORE.

Sign up for the Harlequin e-newsletter and
download a free book from any series at
TryHarlequin.com.

CONNECT.

Join our Harlequin community to share
your thoughts and connect with other
romance readers!
Facebook.com/groups/HarlequinConnection

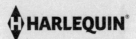

**ROMANCE WHEN
YOU NEED IT**

HSOCIAL2018